SWADESH:

THE AGE OF STARTUPS

S RAGHUNANDANA

NOTEBOOK
PUBLISHING

First published in 2019 by Notebook Publishing,
20–22 Wenlock Road, London, N1 7GU.

www.notebookpublishing.co

ISBN: 9781913206215

A CIP catalogue record for this book is available from the British Library.

Typeset by Notebook Publishing.

To my parents and my wife

PROLOGUE

Our country is rich in natural resources, but, although available in abundance, it is not optimally utilised, a considerable percentage of people within our country facing a serious struggle to earn their daily bread.

After some time in this area, we can witness some who are entirely acclimatised and comfortable with the chores of day-to-day life—and, conversely, we can also perceive several of those indulging in deviant, unethical behaviour as a result of their greed. Life is a combination of the good and the bad, a balance of yin and yang, with hurdles dotted throughout, opportunities taken and missed.

Indeed, amongst all of this food for thought, failure can be viewed as the stepping-stone of success: struggles shape us, and life, in all its struggles and splendour, is a one-time opportunity—one in which the most must be made of, rather than expecting all to simply fall into one's lap.

In this world filled with both structure and chaos, I am ambitious: I dream of a better life, to alter conventions and practices we long since should have outgrown. The first step towards my aspiration: to make fictitious work non-fiction.

Life's colours, in all their vibrancy, have forever fascinated me, and it is whilst penning this novel that I feel confident in the belief that my readers will be happy to oblige in accompanying me on this journey—one in which I have endured and wish to reflect on.

Swaraj is the hero of our story here, and it is this story that incorporates all the driving forces—all the people and emotions—that played a pivotal role in moulding him—Swaraj's so-called 'Swadesh'. It is whilst ignited by such elements that he restarts his life, one liberating him from the whims and fancies of others, one centring on the truth within him, one that will act as a source of inspiration for anybody facing confusion and disorder.

CHAPTER ONE

Our scene opens on Akshaya Thrithiya, a very auspicious day within the Hindu calendar. Despite the air being warm and muggy, the God of Rain cast a summer shower to welcome the arrival of a Saga: a hero to be.

The lounge of the hospital in which we begin was full. It was May 15th, 1991. A room filled with anxious minds waited in apprehension, the very walls seeming to be waiting with bated breath. It wasn't long before the doctor emerged to announce the news of the new arrival into the family: a baby boy.

Upon hearing the news, the infant's father seemed to glow from within with immense pride and joy, his ecstasy seemingly spreading to his relatives and friends, who, in a ring of happiness and fulfilment, stood beside him. Mr Keerthy Raj had become a father for the second time. His second son was to be named Swaraj.

The surrounding individuals were all family and friends of the family stemming from both the maternal and paternal side of the family, all of which chattering amongst themselves contentedly, exchanging friendly greetings and distributing treats—and, at the centre of it all, the proud parents glowed with silent pride. The obstetrician—Dr Sudha—was thanked for all his assistance, and wishes of health and happiness were bestowed upon the mother and child.

Swaraj's brother—five years his senior and named Vaibhav—gazed upon his younger brother with love and curiosity, and, though perhaps overly possessive in the well-meaning way older siblings often are, he welcomed the extension to his family, embracing the status of 'older brother' with open arms.

All these happenings occurred within a fraction of a minute; reams of individuals admiring the beautiful child before the nurse arrived, removing the infant from Sunaina's arms—the mother completely stricken—and bundling him in a blanket. Brows furrowed, Keerthy Raj addressed the nurse, 'Where do you think you're taking my son?'

The nurse gently explained: this had been a premature delivery, and the infant required intensive care and observation. He would have to remain in an incubator for a few days before he could go home with his family—just a few days, she reassured, and assuming all was well, both mother and baby would be discharged and free to go and resume life.

It is worth noting here, as a form of background for Keerthy Raj, that he had previously formulated a schedule whilst on his way back from the office one day, detailing how he was to take care of his children whilst balancing work life—including frequent walks in nature and time slots in which he could assist his wife.

The reader may also find it of use to note that Mysore—the cultural capital of Karnataka—is a famous historical place situated in India, such a mythological reference linking back to the puranas, which has described the glory of the goddess Chamundeshwari. The legend follows she incarnated in this place, with the purpose of killing the demon named Mahishasura. Thus, she is referred to as Mahishasuramardini.

Every Mysorean is indebted to Mahishasuramardini, and regard her with respect, sincerity, and reverence. Indeed, from this, we can regard Mysore as a place where culture, tradition, and heritage are all intertwined with the lives of its wards—forming a city of true beauty and wonder.

CHAPTER TWO

The years rolled by, and Swaraj was a toddler no more, and, as in the case of any given parent, Mr and Mrs Keerthy Raj had strong, solid visions for their children: they wanted them to be well- cultured, disciplined, educated, and it is with this goal in mind that they cared for their children rigorously, closely monitoring their growth (both physically and mentally) and providing a wealth of sweet treats—chocolates and chips being a particular favourite amongst the infants—as a sign of constant appreciation and recognition of their children's' many attributes and talents.

Mr and Mrs Keerthyraj were officials; hence, their children were often cared for by their grandparents, a wealth of their days being passed in granny's house—all the locals being in agreement that Grandmother Poorvi was more than a mother. Their uncle—a rather paternal fellow—also harboured a strong attachment—particularly to Swaraj—, and thus would do everything in his power on a daily basis to ensure he was happy.

A chubby child with a wide smile and rich dark complexion, Swaraj, in his adult years, would reflect on his childhood with pure joy and appreciation, and, like a tape recorder, he would flip through the contents of his memory, filled with impossible volumes of love, gifts, and wishes of health and prosperity.

In what felt like the blink of an eye, 25 years elapsed—and it was during this time that a private-sector bank had organised an award presentation ceremony.

The heat a heavy, stifling blanket draped across the room, the auditorium was jam-packed, heaving with individuals all both anxious and eager for the ceremony, the air alive with the buzz of conversation: their views and anticipation, their expectations and concerns. The air was thick, and the people tense.

There was one individual in amongst the throng that is the focus of our narrative. As per the schedule, the guests occupied the expanse of the stage, an impossible amount of individuals streaming through the main doors by the minute and filling the space. Our guest of concern had arrived with an objective in mind: to announce the name of the year's Star Performer.

It was directly after such an announcement that the air began to crackle with thunderous applause, whistles piercing the commotion. The name was 'Swaraj', and the audience in its entirety quickly arose: a standing ovation to their winner. Swaraj's cheeks burned with pride and shyness as he journeyed to the stage to collect his achievement: this was representative of It his sincerity and dedication within his profession, and, although his modesty would never allow him to utter such a notion to himself, the title was much deserved, his dedication within the workplace unmatched by any of his fellow colleagues.

As one would likely expect, this ended up being a highly memorable day in Swaraj's life: any photo taken from that day could testify to the fact that he was flustered and speechless for its entirety, the Managing Director of the bank giving him a tight handshake in appreciation and recognition. Swaraj was in the limelight, the hero of the day in everyone's eye, and it was at the conclusion of the ordeal that Swaraj conveyed his gratitude to all who had accompanied him in his academic journey. Of course, his family had all attended this event to commemorate Swaraj's successes, and all seemed to swell with pride as each of their names were uttered at the podium.

Piercing this veil of happiness and positive regard for Swaraj, the Branch Manager lingered in the background, unsettled: indeed, he had noticed Swaraj's rapid growth within his career—quicker than most—, and yet hadn't particularly viewed him as a threat until now. A threat he didn't welcome.

Swaraj remained, however, in blissful oblivion to this: life seemed very beautiful and promising, with a warm, committed wife who seemed to share the same mind as him. He had married young—shortly after his 24th birthday—, and yet thus far, the marriage had proven deeper, more successful, more loving, than most commencing late into adulthood. He had married for love, and it was this love that had served him well.

Overall, we can say that Swaraj's life was running rather smoothly: he had never been afraid of going against the norm in order to serve himself better— whether that be in terms of the circumstances of his marriage, or the rate at which he had progressed in work—, and it was these choices that had paved the way for his current sense of fulfilment.

This contrasted highly with the lives his parents had led: his mother was a government servant, and his father a Senior Accountant in a factory. Such occupations were consuming and tiring, and led to both parents, despite their constant attention to their children, fighting such high amounts of exhaustion that the demands of their sons every morning only added to this mass burnout. Swaraj, as a small child, had yearned for his mother, but in vain. In his infancy, he would commence each morning at 8:30am, wolfing a sweet Pongal for his breakfast before arriving at a nearby nursery, accompanied by his brother. He was rather average in terms of his academics— although he admittedly did find enjoyment in such ventures—, and the school day would pass in quick succession, arriving back at home at the same time as their parents, as was the daily routine for many years.

Padma, the school maid, grew rather attached to Swaraj, and had been the one to console him during his first few days at nursery, aiding him in his gradual acquaintance with the school atmosphere.

Alongside his brother, Swaraj's cousin, Srushti, accompanied him throughout his schooling. They were the same age and so played together on a daily basis, and it was during one such day of play that Swaraj, playing animatedly beside a full water tank, tripped and fell into the water—and, unable to swim, thrashed beneath its surface in terror. It was Padma who had noticed, leaned into the water's edge, and lifted him out, wrapping him in a towel and drying his hair and tears.

Though chilling at the time, it is incidents such as these that form the framework of our childhoods, in all its charm and ultimate nostalgia. It is whilst in childhood that we yearn for the title and social standing of adulthood, and it is in adulthood that we reflect on our childhoods and yearn for such freedom and simple contentedness.

CHAPTER THREE

Swaraj relished his time with his friends throughout his studies: he favoured both creative play and practical work, and can recall an incident in nursery when the full class fought for a single bicycle brought to their class.

At the conclusion of their nursery days, Swaraj, Srushti, and Vaibhav were admitted to a school near their grandparents', their daily routine involving one another at every step: at each ring of the school bell, Vaibhav would come to collect Swaraj whilst Srushti waited for both of them at the class door, the trio ensuring one another's arrival to class, hands held, bond strong.

It was at 4pm on a cool afternoon that the school's last bell rang, and, as usual, Vaibhav arrived outside Swaraj's class to accompany him home-only to find nobody was in the classroom besides the teacher—who, noticing the child's panic, informed him that all parents had been told to come into school and collect the children themselves, and that she had just seen his brother in the playground.

Now accompanied by Srushti, Vaibhav went in search of Swaraj: initially in the playground, and, when unsuccessful, in each of his classrooms, in all the boys' toilets, and even in his teachers' stockrooms—all in vain. Panic uncoiling in their stomachs and tears inadvertently beginning to roll down their cheeks, they were gripped by desperation, their minds beginning to jump ahead to the near future: how would they tell their grandparents?

Face pale and eyes wide in fear and anxiety, Vaibhav had no choice but to go back to his grandparents', as his parents had taken on an extra shift and wouldn't be arriving home till late.

Of course, the boy's worries did not go unnoticed, and it wasn't long before he was confronted by his grandmother, the knot twisting in Vaibhav's gut coming undone at his grandmother's concern and all his emotion breaking loose. His shoulders shook and tears once again trailed down his face, and his voice wavered as he said, 'We couldn't find Swaraj anywhere in school.'

To his surprise, Vaibhav's grandmother simply smiled, rubbing his shoulders reassuringly and explaining that Swaraj had come home himself in the afternoon, and was currently playing in the neighbour's garden. Vaibhav was taken aback and Swaraj was called back home before being lectured on his not informing his brother and cousin of his early departure.

Swaraj was a rather average student, but harboured a deep passion for sports and writing: even in his infancy, he would pen short stories and poetry, later directing his innovation toward drawing and painting—pieces that were ultimately appreciated and admired by his friends.

Meanwhile, Keerthyraj had built a new house within a developing area a far distance from their grandparents' house—and, upon its completion, the family's routine shifted significantly, for both the parents and the children.

CHAPTER FOUR

Class X is a milestone in every student's life, and, as any of my family and childhood friends could attest, science and mathematics were not my cup of tea, my scorings in such subjects an inevitable eyesore to both myself and my parents—myself because I wanted to pass these subjects in my very first attempt.

To add salt to the wound, exams were fast approaching, and it was as my worries surrounding such an event increased that I began to spend the majority of my time with all the Gods, in the hopes that they would take special care of me. Even in my dreams, I envisioned them standing in a queue, eager to shower me with their blessings.

'Ahh, yes, Swaraj,' they would say, noting my unease. 'Here, let us eradicate your fears.'

As one may expect, exams both approached and were over in quick succession, and, before long, my results were posted to the board, in black and white for the world to see: nowhere to hide.

Upon reviewing the board, my parents visibly shivered—but not for the reason I would have expected. Riddled with anxiety and praying that my pleas for success had been answered, I examined the board and found, to my utter shock, that my name was there, on the First Class category.

It was a victorious moment, my parents and close relatives both elated and baffled at my success: my brother Vaibhav had, of course, always been a high-rank student, and it had been from a very young age that I had been dubbed a 'struggler'. I had shocked everyone—myself included.

Having applied to a variety of colleges in time for my graduation, I received a letter of acceptance shortly after the release of my impressive grades at a highly reputable college. The first few days in the college were admittedly horrifying, but it wasn't long before a group of seniors took me under their wing and welcomed me cordially. Within a few weeks, everything seemed to be in good order, and, amidst the hectic hours within the classroom—featuring an expanse of unstimulating lectures and lethargic tasks—, we friends always ensured we did something memorable each day.

It was during one such day that I attended a new placement being conducted on-campus, and, whilst making my way to the classroom, I noticed a girl dashing to the same room as me. As much as I couldn't make out her features in the split second I'd seen her, a gut instinct told me to wait for her—an instinct I gave in to.

Thus, I waited in front of the room, and, as the session was about to finish, the girl, surely enough, emerged, accompanied by a friend. For a moment, it felt as though my heart had stopped, and I had the momentary urge to drop all the day's demands and trail after her.

From the direction she was heading, I could see she was leaving the college grounds, this realisation causing a pang of regret to my chest. I ran to the gate and, after a few minutes elapsed—perhaps more—, I heard a vehicle skidding beside me. Turning towards the sound, I saw a car struggling to come to a stop and, to my horror, could make out the object of my desire in the driver's seat through the windshield.

It was in this moment that I made the snap decision to murmur a prayer: for the Gods to give me a chance to marry this girl—although I highly doubted this prayer would come to fruition considering I had thus far been unlucky in all aspects of my life, all my wants being a struggle to obtain, big or small.

It was shortly after this incident that, after completing the remainder of my exams and undergoing the necessary training, I was placed at one of the top positions within a prestigious compartment of the Pvt Sector Bank. However, it is important to note that I was permitted a week off before commencing training—a week I spent in Bendakaluru with my cousins.

It was after this much-needed break that I went to the training institute to begin my classes. It was whilst waiting for my trainer to arrive that I was introducing and familiarising myself with my future colleagues—and, whilst doing so, a sound came from the door beside me. All seemed to happen in slow-motion from that moment: one second I had been jovially conversing with my colleagues, the next there she was, the girl who had been in the accident all those weeks before. I felt like a king, a god, and it was in that moment that I swore to myself that I *would* marry this girl—nothing in the world could stop me.

Like an angel, like a siren, she approached me, searching for a space to occupy as there was no more on the front row. She reminded me of the women in advertisements—untouchable, ethereal—, and it was here that my imagination wandered as I sat beside her. She turned towards me, extended her hand and gave me a handshake. I was entranced and, as she told me her name, I felt in a crazed stupor, captivated by the contours of her face, her eyes, her lips. Her face was like a full moon, bright and inducing feelings of wonder, her eyes like two stars in the dark sky. Her lips were rose, her nose angled, her chin a sunflower.

Breaking the spell, it was at this moment that our trainer finally arrived. She turned her heavenly face away from mine and surveyed the trainer—something I felt was an impossibility to do at this point. I angled my face towards her and, as she concentrated on the trainer's word, I watched her, taking in her purple top and black leggings, the freckles dotted across her nose, the length of her lashes.

Thankfully, the first day of training was short—just an introduction and induction to the course. It was a little later, whilst stood in the car park, that I found myself searching for her: she will, I reasoned, have arrived in her car.

One scan of the road and I found her: she was clearly waiting for somebody. This, I thought, could be my opportunity to propose to her. She was beautiful, and would draw the attention of other men if I didn't lay down my claim quickly.

However, just as I was about to approach her, a man beat me to it: mid-fifties, perhaps, with greying hair and similar features to her. She smiled and embraced him: clearly her father.

The next day, I arrived at the training institute bright and early. Notorious for always running late, this was a novelty for me, and yet here I was, dawn barely breaking over the horizon, bouncing restlessly on my toes in the hopes of spotting the object of my desire: she seemed the type to arrive early.

As it happened, I was right: only a few minutes after me she entered, smiling as she noticed me. As I sat beside her and started to make light conversation, I realised something: I was already very possessive of her, a physical shudder running down my back as the thought of another male sitting beside her. She looked beyond beautiful, as always, and it was here that I finally properly introduced myself, asking if I could have the pleasure of knowing her name.

She smiled, creases forming around her beautiful mouth and her eyes lighting up. 'My name is Avani.'

At this point, people were slowly beginning to drift in, and before long the place was full, electrified with excitable chatter. Here, I was formally introduced to Avani's friends, and it was upon our trainer's arrival that we were all put into a group of eight for the day's group activities.

Altogether, there was a total of twenty-four people in the session, fourteen of which (myself included) being boys, the remainder girls. Of course, Avani was the one who had captured my heart—but, according to one of her friends, there was another who had taken a liking to me.

A few days later—on the day of our first test—, I noticed a girl stand beside me, and I quickly introduced myself to evade any potential awkwardness. She then told me her name—Shwetha—before elapsing into silence, mutely studying my face. I ignored this and continued with my work, at one point stopping to ask for an answer to a question—only to find she was still steadily surveying me. She remained silent despite my question, as though she were deaf, and was slightly smiling to herself, as though harbouring a secret nobody else knew. I smiled at her uneasily and finished my test, rising to leave. A few steps later and it was clear I had a shadow: Shwetha was silently following me and, after a moments, stopped.

'How was your test?'

Surprised by her sudden question, I responded that it had gone well. As though I hadn't responded, she then asked for my phone number, which I gave to her, confused. She thanked me, skipped away, and turned a corner. Shaking my head in bafflement, I headed home.

Barely an hour elapsed before I received a message: *It was nice seeing you today — Your close friend.* Clearly, it was Shwetha. Mind blank, I did not respond to the message, and it was then that I received another, this time from my friends suggesting a game of football. Leaving my phone at home, I shrugged on my coat and headed outside.

A few hours later, after countless games, I arrived home and, upon checking my phone, found I had twenty missed calls and messages climbing into the hundreds. A quick scan of just a handful of the messages made one thing pretty clear: Shwetha was in love with me.

For the remainder of the day, my mind remained blank: I had no idea how to even begin to respond to such a large amount of heartfelt messages. Thus, I continued with my evening as normal, a couple of hours later making some dinner and settling down to watch some TV.

The news channel started playing automatically, their main story being that of a young girl who had just committed a suicide. Disturbed both by the story and the day's events, my night was plagued with insomnia, and it was evident very quickly that I would not be getting any sleep anytime soon. It was because of this that, despite it being in the early hours, I messaged Shwetha back: *Goodnight.* Pretty much the instant that I had pressed Send I received a response: *Goodnight, dear.*

It was from that moment, my mind fogged with fatigue and confusion, that I made a decision: I would sleep with her the following day. As if by magic, I then fell asleep, dreams filled with Avani and what I envisaged our future together to be.

The following day, determined to stick to my decision, I approached Shwetha, who immediately opened her mouth, no doubt to commence a lovers' spiel.

I held a finger up to halt her. 'Before you start,' I murmured, 'let me give you some clarity: I don't like you, and, as a matter of fact, I'm in love with another girl.' Right on cue, Shwetha's face turned ashen. I pushed on. 'I know you're a good person, and perhaps we would have been compatible, but I trust my heart.'

Her eyes brimming with pure, unbridled emotion, she nodded and thanked me delicately. 'Can I just ask you something?' she murmured, staring up at me with wide, doe-like eyes. 'Can you promise me that if your lover decides to marry another, that you'll come back to me?'

Knowing full well in my heart that this would never be the case, I shrugged and nodded: no harm done. She exhaled shakily, thanked me again, and made me promise not to delete her number, swinging out the door towards the car park.

Guilt wrapped itself around my gut like a snake: I had been the object of a girl's heartbreak. Troubled, I went back home, a chill seeming to have settled itself beneath my skin—eventually leading to intense aches and pains. Downing some medicine, I got an early night, awakening the following morning feeling even worse than before: clearly, I would not be able to go to training.

Shortly after awakening I received a message from Shwetha asking why I hadn't arrived. I sleepily tapped back a brief explanation of my illness, adding that I needed to get some more sleep.

Take care, dear, was her instantaneous response. Mildly irritated, I responded: *Please don't call me 'dear'. I need to rest now.*

Despite my sleeping for the majority of the day, the following morning, my throat was sorer and my head more fogged than before. I wouldn't be going to training again.

However, as the sun reached its highest point in the sky at noon, I felt a slight improvement in my health. I knew I should just go to class: perhaps having something to do would just snap me out of this sickness.

It was as I started to get ready for the day that nausea began churning in my gut—and it was nothing to do with the illness. I was wracked with anxiety—anxiety directed, I realised, at seeing Shwetha. *What are you being so silly for?* I lectured myself, annoyed at my own reaction. *Everyone experiences this situation at some point. This is not the way to react. Breathe.*

Upon arriving at class, I took a seat, mentally saving the one next to me for Avani. However, right on cue, it was Shwetha, not Avani, that took her place. I felt a pang in my chest and quickly rose from the seat, sitting next to where Avani had just sat. Shwetha's cold, icy gaze followed me as I took the seat and leaned back, as though I were a villain, a murderer.

CHAPTER FIVE

The last week of training comprised wholly of hands-on sessions on the core banking software—an area I excelled at, having passed all such levels with a minimum of 90%. Indeed, I had been my friends' primary mentor in this area. It was whilst halfway through such a level a couple of days later that Shwetha approached me.

'Could you help me with this?' she asked, cocking her head to the side. 'I can't complete the level.'

Inhaling deeply, I nodded. 'Because I consider you as a friend,' I responded. 'Nothing more.'

To my surprise, she laughed heartily. 'And I'm *asking* you as a friend.' She shrugged. 'I have a boyfriend now, and he's nothing like you. He loves me a lot.'

It was as though the weight of the world had suddenly been taken off my shoulders. I beamed, and began jumping on the spot, expressing my happiness for her and completing the rest of her level with my face aching from smiling.

And it was from that point that all seemed to start falling into place. Every day after class, our gang would sit on the roadside and pass the time chatting—our newfound routine.

It was during one such day that the topic of first crushes arose. I started telling everyone about her crush—about Avani, without stating her name—, and, as Avani began to speak, listing all the things she loved about this mystery man, I felt my own anxiety rising in my throat: perhaps she was already committed to somebody, or engaged to be married.

After a week of nerves and overthinking, I asked her for her number, which she happily gave to me. It was also on the same day that I found her on my main social media account and started to explore her details, including her friends list and the comments on her statuses and photos. After such investigating, it seemed safe to conclude that she was not engaged and was single. With this in mind, I decided it was time to at least try to win her over.

The following day, when we had finished our training, we all met at our main hangout spot and began to wander round. It was when boredom struck that we all decided to go to a local famous garden in Mahishapura, some of us—myself included—having brought their bikes. Avani not having brought hers, I offered her to sit on the back of mine. She agreed, her hands wrapped around my stomach as we sped through the bustling streets and to the garden, my heart in my mouth and my head in the clouds: this was happiness. The day in the garden was passed joyfully: photos were taken and games were played.

The following day, it was decided that we would meet at Avani's place at 10:00. Having arrived early, I was waiting outside for the others to arrive when Avani emerged and, smiling, invited me inside.

It was after some small talk between myself and her that she led me to the living room and introduced me to her parents: her father, Rajesh, and mother, Sridevi.

'Would you like a drink?' she asked, her face seeming to glow. She could have passed as an angel.

'I'll have whatever you're having.'

She dipped her head and headed to the kitchen. It was from here that her father began enquiring about my background, and it was whilst answering, my heart illuminated with hope, that I wondered if this meant her parents would approve of me as a potential husband. However, it wasn't long before these hopes were diminished: he quickly clarified it was just something he referred to as 'KYC Formalities'. Unable to keep my emotions at bay, my eyes began to fill with tears and, as Avani re-entered, she stated, 'I don't want to marry now; I need a year's time.'

Any given parents want their daughter to marry a well-settled man, oftentimes neglecting what it is their hearts say. It was after I had left her house later that day that I began reflecting on this conversation with her parents and understanding their perspective a little more: after all, I hadn't even started my career yet, nor did I yet have a bank balance to propose to her.

It was some time later that we all received a call regarding training from the institute: our placement results had been released. My heart pounding against my ribcage, I silently prayed that Avani would be placed in the same branch as me.

My track record of bad luck, however, remained consistent here: God did not listen to my pleas, my appointment letter stating that my new place of work was in collaboration with Ravanapuram—over 250 miles away from my current place.

The following morning after my receipt of such news, myself and my close friend, Satish, arrived at the railway station to book the tickets for our journey: he had been appointed for Dhatri, which was close to Ravanapuram. At this point, my feelings were split between happiness at a new beginning and sadness at leaving my family and my roots.

Everybody from training had been allocated to their respective program, with the exception of Avani: her placement had been put on hold. A few days before we were due to leave, everybody met and wished one another good luck, exchanging hugs, treats, and warm farewells.

Finally, the day of departure had arrived: all my possessions had been packed in just one bag, and I was ready to leave my home. My goodbye to my parents had been emotional, and it wasn't long before my friend arrived to drop me off at the railway station.

It was whilst we were on the way that, gripped by impulse, I hurriedly asked my friend to take a detour so I could visit somebody important and, within half an hour, I had met up with her and received her parents' blessings. It was whilst myself and my friend continued our journey to the station that my friend asked who she was.

I remained quiet for some time before responding. 'She is my future wife.'

His expression was priceless. I smiled, gave him a hug, and entered the station, not looking back.

CHAPTER SIX

TEN YEARS LATER

The new government had taken an oath and, as a result, an overwhelming number of people were facing the impacts of a food drought—even those within major cities. The CM was silent on the issue, failing to put forward a proper solution.

It was on one fine day that an individual contacted his friend for the solution to this problem. It was from here that he was introduced to Swaraj, who proceeded to explain his views and plans in eradicating this issue. Hearing of such a solution, it wasn't long before the CM contacted him, offering him a price for such a solution. Unexpectedly, Swaraj turned down such an offer without a second thought.

'Please, I do not want any money. Just support for my work.'

The CM, confused but happy, proceeded to ask why. Swaraj's laugh sounded down the line.

'Some people are not concerned about the people—but I am.'

The CM worker was speechless, and Swaraj promptly hung up. Finally taking the phone away from his ear and snapping out of his reverie, he then went to his car, his Personal Assistant—who had been listening in on the phone conversation—tailing him.

'Shall we kill him?' the PA enquired casually. 'He has lot of attitude, and he doesn't care for you.'

The CM worker shook his head. 'Wait for some time; let him do whatever he wants to do. We'll decide what to do with him later.'

Meanwhile, Swaraj was approaching his own car, having packed his bag, a photograph clutched in his left hand. He got into his car and began to stare at the photo, his eyes brimming with tears.

He started his car and, as he began to drive, his mind wandered to his past: the people in it, the highs and lows, the many memories he had come to acquire. It was whilst pondering such things that Swaraj suddenly realised he had lost control of his car. In a matter of seconds, he plunged into a field and jumped from the vehicle, the car skidding further into the field and flipping over before coming to a halt. Delirious with the pain of the injuries he had received from the impact of his landing, Swaraj slipped out of consciousness.

A few hours later, the clouds darkened and it began to rain heavily, the drops like blades with how cold they were. Swaraj shortly regained consciousness and, trying to get up, found he couldn't: he was far too badly injured.

Panic and desperation beginning to pump through his veins, it wasn't long before Swaraj could make out a figure approaching him. His name was Chandru and, noting the wreckage of the car and Swaraj dipping in and out of consciousness, quickly came to Swaraj's aid, bundling him in the back of his own car and taking him to the clinic. Here, he was given potentially life-saving treatment, and was discharged just a few days later, Chandru having remained by his side for the entirety of his stay.

Both were introduced to one another, and, after some light conversation, Swaraj asked if Chandru would be happy to have him as a houseguest for some time whilst he dealt with his affairs.

'I'd be happy to,' Chandru responded. 'We'll begin our house-hunt from tomorrow.' Chandru thought for a moment before adding, 'Although my place may be a little adjustment for you: we currently don't have any water because of the draught.'

With that, they arrived at his residence and, the hour being late, Chandru quickly provided Swaraj with a mat and bedsheet before retiring to his own bedroom.

The following morning, achy but well-rested, Swaraj arose, murmured a morning prayer, and wandered to the kitchen. Chandru promptly offered him some fresh milk, which he gulped down gratefully before heading to the lake a few minutes' walk away for a bath.

Upon returning—slept, fed, and bathed—, Swaraj addressed his newfound companion.

'I need to speak to you, Chandru,' he began. Both men took a seat before Swaraj continued, 'I want you to help me and stay with me until I have completed my work.'

Chandru nodded slowly, thinking in silence for a moment. 'What *is* your work? And why did you choose to come here, instead of going back home?'

'My intentions are good,' Swaraj reassured his friend, noting his apprehension. 'I am looking for a village that doesn't have any of its basic necessities, and I want to make that village an example for the remaining villages. The CM has approved of my doing these things, and I would like your help in this regard.'

Chandru shook his head in disbelief. 'Have you actually gone mad? Do you really think this would be *easy*? You're telling me you've been approved by the government, and yet you should no matter than to believe such people: all they care about is money and power. Don't waste your time.'

Swaraj, to Chandru's annoyance, started to laugh. 'I understand what you're saying,' he responded, 'and I respect your words. But think of the people who don't have *anything*, who sacrifice their lives to serve food for the wealthy. We have to respect them and provide them with a more sustainable solution—death not being the ultimate solution.'

Chandru eyed Swaraj levelly. 'In that case, you came to the right place. Quite frankly, none of our needs are met here: all the people in the village go to cities to earn their weekly wages, and nobody wants to stay here. Farmers are unable to grow their crops because of the lack of water, also leading them to be unable to pay their outstanding bank loans.' He shook his head. 'Suicide rates are at an all-time high as people can't live with the guilt of not being able to take care of their families.' He took a pause. 'And you think you can just *solve* this?'

Swaraj nodded without a moments' hesitation. 'Even the government has given up on fixing it, but if you help me, we both can do it.'

Chandru was still sceptical and yet found himself smiling at the prospect of being able to do such good. Swaraj continued, 'What's the name of this village?'

'Ramagiri.'

Swaraj nodded. 'Shall we meet with the head of the village? We can ask them of their plans and views about all this.'

'We can try,' Chandru shrugged. 'Although I wouldn't get my hopes up, if I were you.'

The twosome planned to meet the head the following day, and the rest of the day elapsed in cheerful conversation and relaxation.

CHAPTER SEVEN

It hadn't felt like it had been a moment since their conversation about their plan when they walked over to the head's residence. Upon arrival, they found three members of the council sat under a banyan tree, chatting and playing some form of card game. Swaraj almost laughed in dismay.

'All these upper-class people who are supposed to be stopping the economy from crumbling, and here they are, playing games and wasting time.'

Chandru didn't respond; instead, he had turned white and suddenly looked wracked with fear. 'Let's not do this,' he said quickly, going to turn back. 'They won't agree with your ideas and we could get in trouble.'

Swaraj simply smiled and headed over to the trio, introducing himself casually and warmly. Before he could say anything more, Chandru interjected.

'Swaraj wants to do some work here, Sarpanch, and he needs your support.'

Sarpanch eyed Swaraj and set down the cards that had been in his hand. 'I know exactly what it is you're wanting to do, and I'll have you know that you will not get any support from our side, nor from this village.'

Swaraj shook his head in disbelief. 'But, sir, please kindly listen to me: I'm not a politician. All I want to do is buy a few acres of land, help along the agriculture here.'

Sarpanch raised an eyebrow. 'Do you know anything about agriculture?' Swaraj nodded and Sarpanch exhaled in defeat. 'You start on the first of next month.' Swaraj felt his heart flutter. 'But I can assure you that if you slack even slightly, I'll have won this fight.' He then turned to address Chandru. 'Call all the farmers, please.'

It wasn't long before the farmers, having received Chandru's update, started drifting in, the whole time Swaraj feeling illuminated with happiness: this was the first step to his ultimate success, to his being able to help humanity.

All the farmers were now gathered and standing before the men, and Sarpanch indicated to Swaraj to take the lead.

'My name is Swaraj, and I want to buy a few acres of land for the agricultural purposes. I'll pay you all whatever price you quote, and, as a thank-you, I'll also offer you employment alongside myself.' The farmers gave away none of their emotions, their expressions remaining neutral. Swaraj suddenly felt nervous. 'If any of you would be willing to take a chance and take me up on my offer, please raise your hand.'

Swaraj waited five seconds, ten, thirty, one minute. Not one farmer raised their hand. Mortified and getting desperate, Swaraj continued, 'If you don't wish to sell at all, perhaps we could look at a five-year lease?'

Again, nobody came forward. Swaraj was about to give up when Chandru cleared his throat and said, 'How about I sell my property for 10lakhs? I also need work.'

After a few moments' pause, one farmer hesitantly raised his hand. Shortly after, another did the same, then another, then another, and, before long, half the farmers' hands had been raised.

In the end, around half of those who had raised their hand agreed for the lease for the land; the others only agreed to the sale. Meanwhile, Sarpanch felt highly on edge: he had very little faith in Swaraj.

'So, what's next?' Sarpanch challenged. Swaraj was unfazed by his almost accusatory tone, and responded without missing a beat. \

'I need to buy a factory; do you have any that are vacant, or planning to be shut down?'

The whole room seemed to pause: none of them knew what to make of this, nor the direction in which Swaraj was heading. Noting everyone's unease, Swaraj swiftly began to his thoughts, his vision. Once he had finished, a few moments of silence elapsed, everybody attempting to digest his words. Could such a plan be a success? Or would it be a waste of time and money?

Finally, one of the farmers spoke up. 'Sir, this is India; nor you or I can change. The politicians will never help us. Such a plan would never gain enough support from those in power. The best thing you can do at this point is go back to wherever you came from.'

The rest of the farmers nodded in silent agreement. Swaraj's chest ached at the man's words, Chandru's face mirroring his own disappointment. Feeling there was no more they could do to help the matter, they nodded in defeat, thanked everyone in the room for their time, and set off back to Chandru's home. Upon arrival, Swaraj noticed a young woman curled on the sofa, drinking tea.

Chandru's face lit up upon seeing her, and he quickly introduced her to Swaraj as Aruna, his wife.

Swaraj tried his best to be cordial, yet he could still feel the light wasn't quite reaching his eyes: he felt wounded after the day's events. After fetching himself a glass of water, Swaraj surveyed the couple before him and attempted a smile.

'You're both made for each other, it seems.'

Chandru smiled, nodded, and kissed his wife on the forehead affectionately. 'You're married also, aren't you?' he returned jovially. 'Please, tell your story!'

At these words, Swaraj's heart sank even lower than before, and, as per Chandru's request, began to narrate his story:

'From the very first time I saw her, I knew I was going to marry her: she was everything I'd ever wanted and more. However, I was transferred to Ravanapuram for work—over 250 miles from her in Mahishapura.

'Upon arrival, I remember how green my surroundings had been, as well as how cold the climate was: I'd arrived in September. It was a semi-urban area—rather underdeveloped. Me and my friend, Satish, whose placement had been close to Ravanapuram, both quickly desperately started miss home. It was during one evening whilst we were reflecting on our times at home that I told him I was planning to marry his close friend, Avani.' Swaraj's voice started to tremble with emotion: it all still felt so raw, so fresh, despite the years that had elapsed. 'He was pissed off for some time, but he eventually came round to the idea, agreeing it'd be for the best and bestowing his best wishes upon us.

'It wasn't long after this confession that I started work, and it was on the morning of my first day that I went to the bank and waited for the Branch Manager, who arrived half an hour later. It was upon his arrival that I gave him my provisional offer letter. Without opening it, he asked me to introduce myself—something I didn't manage to do very professionally, due to my nerves. The BM literally laughed in my face: he claimed I was still in "college mode", that I would not be capable of handling the bank responsibly and that I was thus unfit for this role.' Swaraj exhaled, his breath shaking. 'To justify his decision, he started to explain the workings of the bank, how my attitude should have been towards the work, and what he would have expected from someone like me.

'As soon as I got home that evening, I immediately dialled Avani's number and began relaying day's events to her. She had managed to console me within a matter of minutes, saying I could prove him wrong by showing my positivity and efficiency in the workplace. It was in this moment, whilst I listened to her words, that I now felt certain of everything I suspected before: that we were meant to be together. It was after she'd finished speaking that I told her how better I always felt after speaking with her, and that I felt we would be compatible as a pair.

'She was silent for a few moments, and it was whilst awaiting her response that I felt as though my heart had stopped in my chest. When she spoke again, she said she hadn't heard me properly, that the line had gone dead. I told her it had been nothing, and then quickly said goodbye, my excuse being that I hadn't yet eaten dinner.

'Despite my failed attempt at confessing my feelings to Avani, I began the following day with newfound confidence. Upon arriving at the bank, I was allocated a seat beside Ajay, a senior working in cash operation. It was through Ajay that I learnt how to check the authenticity of cash notes, and, ten days after meeting, he was due to go on leave—meaning I would have to take his place and sit at the counter. He had told me it would be a simple, short-term job, not knowing that on the very first day the cash had not been tallied: there was 500rs difference. For a while, I sat in a state of panic, ultimately informing the manager of the issue. He came to the counter, checked the bundles, noted the same difference I had, and simply told me to solve the issue by checking the bundles.

'Still confused and worried, I went to the vault, wrote the closing cash balance in the register, closed the bank, and left to get some food—after which I called Avani and, again, relayed the day's events. She had been placed at a similar branch in Mahishapura as a Cash Officer, and it turned out she'd had a very similar first day to me.

'It was a few weeks later, whilst having one of our daily calls, that I brought up the topic of marriage. This didn't go down too well: her opinion towards love and marriage was mostly negative, and, no matter how many benefits of marriage I presented her with, she was not convinced.

'It wasn't long after this that I made up my mind to finally confess my feelings to Avani. I dialled her number and, after we had exchanged our usual greetings and relayed how our days had been, I took a breath and quickly asked her not to scold me, to just hear me out. A few fear-filled moments of silence elapsed before I finally said the words I had been wanting to say since I had very first laid my eyes on her: "I want to marry you". I quickly explained that I was certain she was my destiny, and that I had thought for a while that we would make a good couple. After a few moments of silence, to my utter horror, she hung up the phone.

'I tried to call her back, praying that the signal had just given out, and yet my silent pleas were shattered as she rejected each call. After attempting to call her for a fourth time, the number disconnected: my number had been blocked.

'I thought about Avani for the rest of the night, my heart aching more than I ever knew it could. I didn't sleep: instead, I spent the night with my mind racing, occasionally trying to call her again, to no avail. but it was not reachable. I was exhausted and wracked with heartbreak by the end of the night.

'The following morning, exhaustion took over and I somehow managed to sleep. It was from when I woke up, having not eaten for 24 hours by this point, that I called Satish, informing him of my conversation with Avani the night before and asking him to tell her to contact me as soon as possible.

'After some time—what felt like a lifetime—, I received a call from Avani, my heart in my mouth and my whole body shaking with joy and relief at just hearing her voice again. She was speaking as though nothing had happened between us, simply telling me about her day. This both relieved and frustrated me: I'd wanted to have her back in my life, and yet it felt strange to not acknowledge this massive shift between us. After a few minutes of this one-sided small talk, I addressed the elephant in the room, asking why she had disconnected my calls, knowing full well how I felt about her. To my dismay, she brushed off my words, scolding me for getting distracted over such matters: I needed to complete the day's work. We'd talk about such things in the evening.

'As you may expect, that workday dragged, my mind solely focused on the possible outcomes from our call that evening. Finally, when the time came for our call, Avani cut to the chase: she stated that she didn't love me anymore, that we would never be a couple because her parents would never agree to it. She also informed me that her parents had actually arranged her marriage to another man, which was to be conducted the following year. Thus, she said I needed to forget the idea completely, that I needed to focus on furthering my career. I needed to not waste any more time and to work on myself so I could get a better girl than her. As suddenly as she had a few nights before, she then hung up the phone.'

It was here that Swaraj concluded his story, as this was the last he had heard from Avani. Chandru and Aruna exchanged a sad look, and the evening was passed in happier conversation so as to lighten the mood.

CHAPTER EIGHT

The following morning, just as dawn was creeping over the horizon, Swaraj and Chandru went to Sarpanch to chase up their query about the factory and vacant storage place space. Sarpanch responded by giving the duo a contact number of someone who could allegedly help them. Swaraj thanked him, dialled the number, and, after a quick conversation with the man on the other end of the line, it was arranged that they would meet near the Tala lake, opposite to which there being a very old factory—which had, unfortunately, been partially burnt.

Upon arriving at this meeting, Swaraj entered the factory in question and, within a few minutes, had decided to buy it. It was over the course of the next few months that he, accompanied by Chandru, commenced his task of renovating the place, making some work stations, cubicles, and conference rooms on one of the floors, also building a very large storage room on the ground floor.

All of this took a matter of four weeks to complete, after which time he gathered all the farmers and landowners outside the renewed factory. Now, he reintroduced his original offer: for the landowners to give the land to him on a five-year lease, with an agreement to provide them with a job with a fixed salary of 25k per month—along with health insurance.

This time, both groups agreed to the offer except one individual, who asked for the agreement details. They were then listed by Swaraj: a five-year lease of the land, the price of which being fixed at 5lakhs per acre—all of which being invested in Mutual Funds with a five-year 'lock-in' period. All owners would receive a 25k monthly salary, and would benefit from health cover and PF facility.

After this clarification, those who agreed started to sign the paperwork and create bank accounts, also noting their new employee codes. The investors quickly received their statements, and promptly began to work for Swaraj—who had registered the factory and applied for the license needed for him to operate the company. The company's directors were primarily CM, as they were the ones who had granted such a request under the CM welfare fund, and it was this that would be privatised for the entire five-year period. The company was registered as 'Farma India Pvt Ltd'.

Shortly after all of this had been sorted, Swaraj headed to the engineering college and hired some of the students for the software development and digital marketing domains. He also frequently checked in with the farmers, getting to know some of their children, who had been studying in the city, some of which he hired. He put up a fence surrounding the entire plough field and made CCTV surveillances.

It was whilst conducting such changes that some of the neighbouring villagers started to gossip about his endeavours. However, Swaraj ignored this and kept true to his word, providing the farmers with work in the fields and the owners with work as store managers. The workday always commenced at 07:00 and finished at 17:00 for the farmers, the store managers, on the contrary, working on a shift-by-shift basis.

Swaraj partitioned the land into four sections, also splitting the farmers into four groups and assigning them to a fraction of the land accordingly, also allocating a team leader to each group. As one may expect, this largely enhanced not only the efficiency but the quality of the work completed.

Whilst doing all of this, he additionally created the company's software, creating advertisements in social media and local newspapers about their work. Such marketing also lent the way to his receipt of some feedback, through which he learnt that some of his employed farmers had taken loans from the bank and had been unable to repay them. To this, he responded by giving his contact number to each person who had filed complaints, asking them to get in contact.

By 18:00, Swaraj would make all the employees and their families meet in one place, during which time he would educate them on the crops and the wealth these could generate for their futures. Such lessons were a daily occurrence, and he did so with the aim of educating and bring awareness to the financial sector and the most optimal way of handling money. Slowly but surely, the company began to thrive and to generate revenue, and, by the end of the month, the company had credited its salary to the respective accounts. Each and every employee relished in the security and reward of receiving a consistent, predictable income, ultimately boosting their moods and thus making their work more productive.

Indeed, whilst Swaraj was very focused on his career-related endeavours, Avani's words echoed in his mind frequently, disturbing him a lot: he would never forget how he had felt about her, nor how her careless words had injured him.

It was on a fine morning that he received a message stating his generous monthly salary had been sent to his account. Remembering Avani's words to make something of himself just a month before, he dialled her number, only to find the call automatically disconnected. More annoyed than upset, he then dialled for his parents and informed them that he received his salary. Their parents quickly displayed their happiness, his father advising him to create a savings account and plan for higher education. It was with these words that Swaraj's previous pride and happiness halted in their tracks: he wanted to explain his wish to increase his salary credit, as per Avani's wishes, to win her over.

As if he had summoned her, Swaraj received a call from Avani the following morning; however, it wasn't until 08:oo that he saw this due to his phone having been on silent and, to his horror, he found he'd missed five calls from her hours before. He immediately tried to phone her back, but she didn't respond, and, for the rest of his day, he waited for her call, to no avail.

It was whilst he was getting ready for another day on the farm the next morning that one of the farmers, Mr

Ranganath, came to his home and asked for a job: his son, he claimed, was an engineer, and received very good marks in his IT core subjects.

After surveying the boy's results Mr Ranganath had printed, Swaraj nodded in approval. 'His marks are good, but does he have a lot of technical knowledge?'

'Yes, plenty!' Mr Ranganath insisted.

'Then tell him to come to the office for an interview in a few hours.'

It turned out Mr Ranganath was rather desperate for pay: the farmer had pledged his land through the Pvt Sector bank, but hadn't had the abundant harvest he'd expected. He was undergoing a load of financial loss, and was unable to pay his loans to the bank.

Swaraj, as much as he empathised with the poor farmer, also had to acknowledge that this was the position the majority of the farmers were in today. With Mr Ranganath's pleas in mind, he went to the factory and checked the employee categories: there were 200 farmers, 200 store managers, and 100 individuals working in marketing and technology. The only space in the factory allocated for marketing was the storage warehouse, as he had not yet sought a retail store or mobile app.

Shortly after his arrival, the boy came for the interview, his father initially accompanying him before waiting in the foyer. When the boy entered the office, Swaraj noticed he was sweating profusely—unsurprising, considering his entire family's financial state probably relied on his success. Swaraj kindly offered him a seat and a drink of water, both of which the boy accepted gratefully.

The boy took a deep breath and Swaraj begun, opening the interview by asking the boy about his vision. To Swaraj's surprise, the boy answered with confidence, as was the case with every other question Swaraj threw his way. It was this confidence, combined with the passion with which he spoke, that made Swaraj offer him the job as a Process Associate within the company. Instead of dismissing the boy, he then asked him to wait here, calling Mr Ranganath into the room.

The boy rose and offered his father the seat, who took it before turning to Swaraj, both hope and apprehension lit in his eyes. Swaraj gave the letter of acceptance to him, looking him in the eyes as he said, 'One day, he will be the boss here.'

Mr Ranganath's eyes instantly filled with tears, and, placing the letter to the side, enveloped his son in a hug, tears running down his cheeks. One a few minutes had elapsed and Mr Ranganath had dried his eyes, Swaraj then continued by saying with some time, he could also secure a job for his wife. Both men left, their cheeks tear-stained and mouths fixed in a smile, and Swaraj felt his heart warm: at least he had managed to save one family.

Now turning to the future, Swaraj found he wanted to expand the market share of his business, exporting to other countries. It was because of this that he scheduled an urgent meeting with the IT team, during which he explained his plans and instructed them to create an app for the purchase of vegetables items with the GPS access so orders could be tracked and delivered to their respective locations. These services, he added, should be available internationally, and all goods delivered within 48 hours of order placement. He also wanted there to be two payment options to allow for more sales: either online payment, or cash/card at delivery. He wanted this feature to go live from next week.

The room stunned at both the originality and pure ambition in his plans, Swaraj pressed on. 'We'll also need to look into recruiting delivery boys—and we also need to make sure we initially mainly focus on existing vegetable merchants so we can build a positive reputation within the company, and look at expanding from there.'

From here, the rest of the team began to brainstorm the ways in which they could create such features in such a short timescale, also exploring their own ideas concerning the business.

Whilst in the throes of business ventures, Swaraj received an unexpected call from Avani two days later. He had been missing her desperately, and had an urge to express such emotions to her.

All of his feelings he had tried so hard to bury came rushing back, he impulsively proposed to her, and she promptly hung up the phone. Within a minute, she had also sent Swaraj a message: *If you propose next time, you will never hear from me again.* Filled with frustration and dejection, Swaraj ignored the message, turning his phone off so he wouldn't have to think about it anymore.

The following day he paid a visit to the bank: the Branch Manager had told him to made take the cash keys and sit as Head Teller. Swaraj was filled with nerves but tried his best to mask over this, wanting to prove the BM wrong from what he had said all his months ago.

Throughout the day, Swaraj's confidence slowly rose, gradually taking the cash with more confidence and swiftly identifying counterfeit notes with the aid of a UV lamp. The BM watched and became increasingly impressed by Swaraj's evident skill, congratulating him on a successful day of work at closing time.

A couple of weeks elapsed of similar work, and with that brought four new employees for the bank. Having performed consistently well over the course of the weeks, the BM instructed Swaraj to train the new workers whilst they completed their training in this branch: they would later be allocated to a different branch. Swaraj accepted this challenge gratefully and, over the course of the next few workdays, taught the new employees the cash process, oftentimes demonstrating the skills he spoke of to drive his points home.

By the end of the training, all the workers received their IDs and access passwords, the BM satisfied with their work after Swaraj's expertise had been passed onto them: they could all now handle the crowd with ease.

Despite this success, Swaraj's branch was severely understaffed: there was only one cash counter and two people working within it, including Swaraj. This meant Swaraj never had the time for a lunch break, oftentimes also going without breakfast also. He eventually looked back on these times as the 'black days', and he frequently found himself having to lie to his parents whenever they checked in so as to not worry them.

After one such exhausting day, Swaraj received yet another call from Avani, this time informing him that she had finally received her placement, and that she would be working as cashier in the same bank, but in Mahishapura branch. This at least provided Swaraj with some happiness: the thought of Avani being close to him, even if he couldn't have her.

A month elapsed and Swaraj received word that his team in the factory had finalised the requested software, and a meeting was scheduled in Swaraj's office to discuss the further process. The app and website had both been built and now featured Live GPRS tracking for orders, also being programmed to maintain consistent communication with customers via email and messages. Swaraj promptly tested this system himself, installing the app on his own phone, registering his mobile number and, indeed, shortly receiving regular messages from the company concerning offers and updates.

Further, in order to truly test the app's workings, he placed his own order, tracking indeed becoming available upon payment. He also promptly received an invoice, which also detailed the warranty period for the product: valid within one hour of receipt.

After such rigorous testing, Swaraj eventually advised his team that he was happy with the software and its features, the app being extremely handy and user-friendly. It was after the establishment of this confidence that he decided to go live with these new features, training being quickly supplied to the vendors with regard to the application, of which there being 100 vendors in and around the border of the village, only 15 of which staying near the city border.

Initially, Swaraj primarily marketed by referral; this resulted in the vendors being aware of who their regular and loyal customers were, and also led to them being more able to connect with new people. This element of personability to the orders additionally led to a spike in sales.

As such sales grew, the company faced higher and higher demand for its products; thus, to keep clients interested, they ensured to provide the best rates out of all their competitors. Further, due to this high demand, hardly any stock went to waste, leaving an abundance of profit to be collected. The company also instilled special offers to loyal customers, quickly leading to the business truly booming.

As the company's profit rose, Swaraj decided to issue bonuses to every single worker—the equivalent of one months' salary—, and yet from this, Swaraj did not take one single rupee: instead, he stored any remaining money into a mutual fund.

Furthermore, Swaraj implemented a policy whereby all workers should be aware of the goings-on of any meetings, even if they hadn't attended; this, field employees were able to watch back a given meeting through video footage. During one such meeting, Swaraj was informed by the accounting department that the company currently had a surplus of 25cr after deducting the issued bonus from online payments—a figure that raised the eyebrows of everyone in the room. After thanking everyone in the room for all their hard work to produce such an amount, Swaraj stated he would keep the surplus in liquid form, which would likely lead to an 8% increase in the surplus's value.

All seemed happy with this with the exception of one worker, who quickly raised his hand. 'Why don't we just keep the surplus in the bank for safety, rather than in a mutual fund?' he demanded.

'I believe in mutual funds because of my previous experience in the MF market,' Swaraj explained patiently. 'However, I'll never rush into a decision if not all are happy with it, so if anyone still has any further concerns, please let me know.'

The man nodded sheepishly, none of the other workers objecting to this plan: they all trusted Swaraj's judgement.

A few weeks later, due to the effectiveness of this plan, the company had taken over almost all of Ramagiri's land—including that of Sarpanch, who made initially poked fun at Swaraj's ideas.

By the end of the first two years of the company's operation, the company had made a breakeven profit, all the farmers having learned to save their personal money by closing their standing loans.

During this time period, Swaraj and Satish would frequently meet during the weekends, either to just kick about in the local area, or to visit home. Whenever they did the latter, Swaraj would always call everyone in their original friend group during training—including Avani—, and they would all meet somewhere, updating one another on their new lives, exchanging their views and opinions on their current branches, and otherwise making light-hearted conversation till evening. After such endeavours, Swaraj would go back to his family home, spending a couple of hours with his parents before setting back off to Ravanapuram with Satish.

It was after one such day that Swaraj received a call from his father and, upon picking up the phone, found his voice was very low, as though he were anxious or scared.

'What's going on?' Swaraj pressed, his whole body having tensed.

There was a pause on the line before he heard his father dissolve into tears. 'It's your Jaya grandmother,' he said, his voice wobbling. 'She has collapsed; she's got a severe head injury. She's in hospital, and the doctors have said she's still unconscious.'

For the rest of that evening, Swaraj's mind was racing. Sickness sat in a pool in his stomach, and his muscles were quickly achy and sore from tension. He had never been closed to his Jaya grandmother, and yet it still felt like a shock. After some thought, he decided he would book another ticket home to see her, telling his branch manager the next day that he needed to request leave; however, this was denied, meaning the soonest he would be able to visit her would be the following Saturday. Because of this, the week passed painstakingly slowly, all the while him praying his grandmother would be okay.

Finally, on Saturday morning, he packed his things, locked up his house, and commenced the six-hour bus journey—during which time he attempted to read a book but instead, unable to focus, found himself staring out the window in a worried stupor. He reflected on his childhood memories with his Jaya grandmother, now imagining the pain she must be in. It was enough to make him feel like he could be sick.

Finally, upon arrival at his parents' house, he dumped his belongings, sought his father, and, without a greeting, asked him for the hospital address. He had been in the house for all of three minutes before he left again, this time to the hospital.

Ten minutes later, Swaraj arrived, enquiring after his grandmother at Reception, who pointed him in the direction of Ward 5—the closest one to where he now was.

He walked over and paused at the door: what if she looked in pain? What if she had already died?

Reminding himself to breathe in through his nose and out through his mouth, Swaraj entered, drew open the curtain at the foot of her hospital bed, and there she was: his grandmother, sleeping like a baby. She had been in a coma for more than three days—the incident having occurred four days before. She looked at peace, and yet Swaraj's eyes filled with tears: his grandma, usually so full of life, now bedbound, unresponsive to any medication.

Approaching slowly, uncertainly, Swaraj went to the head of the bed and delicately placed a hand on his grandma's forehead, and the tears that had been brimming slowly began to roll down his face.

A few minutes elapsed in this manner before his father entered: clearly he had set off quickly after Swaraj. Taking in the image of Swaraj, inconsolable, his palm pressed against his grandmother's skin, Swaraj's father also started to cry, coming over to where Swaraj was standing and rubbing his back soothingly.

'You need to go to the house and get some rest, Swaraj,' he murmured. 'You've had a long journey.'

Nodding slowly, Swaraj kissed his grandmother where his hand had been and embraced his father before leaving, drying his eyes. True to his word, he went straight back home and fell asleep the second his head hit a pillow, his dreams plagued with images of his grandmother, immobile, stuck in a permanent slumber.

CHAPTER NINE

The following morning, he awoke early and went straight to the hospital, staying by his grandmother's side until the sun had completed its daily cycle. It was as evening arrived that Swaraj remembered his work—something that now seemed like a world away. The weekend was closing, and he hadn't been granted leave from work, meaning he'd have to depart to Ravanapuram soon.

Swaraj squeezed his grandmother's hand, blinked back his tears, and left the ward for the last time.

During his journey back, his heart seemed to be made of lead, weighing down in his chest, aching and throbbing. For the entirety of his journey, he pondered on his grandmother's condition, and his father's words from before he had left: *If her condition doesn't improve soon, we may have to take the decision out of her hands and switch off life support.*

His father had said it mechanically, robot-like, as though his only successful coping mechanism was to push back all his emotions, to deal with everything in a numb, detached manner. It had been more than Swaraj could handle.

Swaraj arrived at work the following morning with a pale complexion and a wandering mind: his disinterest in attending to customers was quickly evident, and this only worsened when his parents ceased to contact him for the two days after his departure. It constantly felt like he was waiting for bad news.

On the third day, however, Swaraj received a call from his brother. 'Have you heard the news?' he demanded as soon as Swaraj picked up the phone.

'No...?'

His brother inhaled deeply, and Swaraj's blood chilled as he realised what was coming next. 'Swaraj, grandma passed away the moment you left the ward on Sunday.' His voice was quivering. 'She's gone.'

Swaraj, suddenly overcome with such a degree of pain he didn't know was possible, hung up the phone and crumbled into tears, curling on the floor, the phone still clutched in his hand.

Less than a minute later, his phone rang again: this time his father. He disconnected the call and messaged him: *I'll call you back.* He felt guilty for ignoring his family, and yet he also needed some time alone to process this. He'd phone them back at the end of the day.

Engulfed with mourning, Swaraj also couldn't help but feel betrayed that his parents and brother had taken so long to tell him. It made him feel like he wasn't a valued member of the family, and it was this, combined with his heartbreak for his grandmother, that left him in a state for the rest of the day.

Later that evening, he reflected further on his childhood: how whenever he was upset, she would be there to tell him a funny story, or a happy story, or one from her own childhood to distract him. She had always been the storyteller of the family.

The day after he had received the news of his grandmother's passing was a holiday, and yet he was not in the mood to visit his friends; instead, he stayed in Ravanapuram, in the end calling Avani and passing the news onto her before breaking down into tears again.

Avani sounded heartbroken at Swaraj's state, and spent the whole call consoling him. It was at the end that, in an act of desperation, Swaraj begged her to accept his love, but, once again, she refused.

'It's not my decision,' she offered. 'My parents already have my future planned.'

It was once they had finished their call that Swaraj realised quite how overwhelmed he felt: by his grandmother's death, by his family's apparent disregard for his feelings, by Avani's rejection. All of this combined made Swaraj wish he could take aa break from work. However, he knew, deep down, that this would be the worst thing he could do: he needed something to hold onto, something in his life he could still control.

Thus, he continued with his work as normal. His investment plan had raised a variety of concerns amongst his workers, but he was confident in its ultimate success.

Further, the app had undergone thorough testing: indeed, everything was well-placed, the app running smoothly, taking in frequent feedback from clients concerning quality control of the vegetables—all of which being positive.

In summary, the majority of Swaraj's focus was on the marketing side of the business, and less on the cultivation process; however, he shortly received a complaint from one of his farmers from the technical team, stating that the land was no longer fertile, so the crops could not be rotated. Such a complaint acting as a wake-up call, he then committed a few workdays to researching the ways in which the land could be made more fertile. Research online and through books not sufficing, Swaraj contacted his friend Vardhaman, who lived as an agriculturist in Australia, asking him for his own advice on the matter. Vardhaman explained that he'd usually have around five harvests a year using chemical fertiliser and sand cleaning to ensure optimal growth. Pointing him in the direction of some resources so Swaraj could understand it better, Swaraj thanked him, hung up, and, with this new knowledge in mind, continued with his research.

Once he was confident he had done all the work he could on the matter, Swaraj arranged for a meeting with the team, during which he showed some footage from Vardhaman's field he had sent him, showcasing the technology and techniques they implemented there. From there, Swaraj echoed Vardhaman's words from their call, explaining the nature and functions of the chemical fertilisers needed, as well as the ways in which they would need to test the quality of the land after every harvest.

All the workers left that meeting filled with optimism at the thought of this new approach, and yet when everything seemed to be going well in the following weeks, there was the constant anxious wait for rain that never came. Raining season started, and yet not a single drop fell, leaving the crops parched.

When the farmers turned to Swaraj for guidance, his mind went blank: never had he predicted such an outcome. He had never felt so unprepared. Whilst the company was still in operation for now, if they didn't harvest more crops soon, they would only be able to afford six more months of salary payments before closing down.

For weeks, Swaraj suffered with extreme insomnia at night as a result of his worries: he had grown this business from nothing, and it now ran the risk of being a failure.

It was during one such restless night that he had an idea: social media. He immediately sat up from where he had been tossing and turning in bed and posted on all of his accounts, stating the company's position and asking for any help anyone could provide. He then tagged every past and present client the company had.

The following morning, he paid a visit to the CM and explained the predicament the company was in. The CM listened, shook his head, and said, 'The best thing you can do is to just close the company so you don't face bankruptcy. It's a lost cause.'

Swaraj's heart sank and, following his own advice, the CM promptly resigned from the company, thus forcing the company to run privately without any government support.

Before long, the drought started to escalate far past simply not raining: now, the nearby lakes and rivers were starting to dry up, any sources of water that had been remaining to the public gone. In turn, the company's storeroom quickly emptied, all potential of harvest having dissipated. In desperation, a number of authorities commenced underground searches for water, to no avail. The company's bank balance plummeted further and further to zero every day, and Swaraj saw the fear in the eyes of his employees. Knowing something needed to be done and the situation addressed, he swiftly organised a meeting with his employees.

At the time of the meeting, all the employees filtered into the room eagerly, awaiting Swaraj's decision as they were sure his calling a meeting meant he had found a way to fix the problem.

Instead, after Swaraj had expressed his happiness and gratitude at them all coming, he turned to the senior farmers and asked, 'How do you think is best to combat this situation?'

The farmers frowned, glancing at one another in confusion before one began speaking. 'I mean... it seems our only option is to wait; wait for the rain god to bless us with some water.'

The room then erupted in chatter, everyone discussing this prospect amongst themselves.

'We should take the land back for ourselves!' one individual shouted out.

'Yes, we've all closed our loans anyway!'

With each new exclamation, Swaraj felt the fear in his eyes growing: he was not ready to lose the company, yet his own team was turning against him. Droplets of water fell to the ground: not from rain god, but from Swaraj's eyes.

CHAPTER TEN

Two weeks had elapsed since Swaraj's grandmother's passing, and he decided to visit home—not because he wanted to see his family, as he was still deeply hurt by their lack of consideration of his feelings, but because he needed to get away from everything at work.

Upon his arrival, he briefly greeted his parents and, despite their objections, went straight to his bedroom and pointedly closed the door. *Good. Let them know how loss feels.*

Swaraj then started unpacking his things and getting ready: he had plans with Avani. Half an hour later, he left without a word to his parents, got on his bike, and sped to her house. Avani had told him that the door was unlocked and so to just let himself in upon arrival, and it was whilst he did so that he noticed there were extra shoes in the porch: Avani's cousin's.

Indeed, as Swaraj started removing his own shoes, he could hear her cousin's voice talking on the phone on loudspeaker. He was laughing jovially when Swaraj heard the voice on the other end of the line say, 'So, what are the bride's details?'

Swaraj's heart seemed to stop for a moment: with all his problems at work, he had forgotten Avani's wedding was today—as a matter of fact, it had likely already happened.

Before he had any time to process this, however, Avani's father appeared and greeting Swaraj warmly, asking after himself and his family.

'Please, take a seat,' he continued, bringing Swaraj inside. 'The groom's family is now arriving to see Avani.'

It was at this moment that Avani emerged from her room, and Swaraj was immediately rendered speechless: her hair pulled back revealing her heavenly bone structure, she wore a Saffron silk saree and smelled of jasmine. She looked like a goddess, and, as Swaraj took in her beauty and realised she would now never be his, tears filled his eyes.

Unable to stand it, Swaraj left the room, stalked out the door, pedalled home, and threw himself onto his bed, not emerging until the sun had set and the other occupants of the household were asleep. It was then that he received a call from Satish, reminding him of his train journey back, his train departing in half an hour.

Repacking his things quickly and leaving for the train station, Swaraj arrived just as the train was about to pull away from the platform. He found his seat reservation, next to which Satish was sat: he had been visiting home, too.

Upon seeing Swaraj, Satish frowned. 'Swaraj! Why do you look so sad?'

Suddenly, Swaraj burst into tears, inconsolable and unable to stop. Satish tried to calm him down, but in vain: Swaraj was a broken man.

Once he had managed to calm down a little, Swaraj said, 'Avani is married as of today. I'm going to resign from work tomorrow; I'm too lost at the moment to be good for anything.'

With that, he began crying again, and continued to do so for the rest of the long journey. True to his word, he went to the bank the following morning and filled a resignation form, requesting leave for a day on top of this considering he was completely overcome with fever as a result of the previous day's stress.

The following day, Satish called him to check on his health and wellbeing, and Swaraj was grateful for being in his thoughts. The following day saw a great improvement in his health, the day off work having done him good; and, as a month rolled by, his notice period was coming to a close and his last day of work was imminent. It was on this day that Swaraj finally called his father and informed him that he had quit work, and that today was his last day.

'But whatever will you do from tomorrow?' his father asked, perplexed.

Swaraj thought for a moment. 'I might take a short break from any work and plan for a professional course.'

Swaraj's father was weary of his decision, particularly when it came to the prospect of finding a wife, but expressed his support regardless, and said he would relay the information to his mother.

It was after this phone call, when Swaraj's future seemed so unstable and uncertain, that he decided to take a walk; and it was whilst he was walking through the streets that he heard voices ahead. Curious, he followed the sound, to find, to his utter shock, the majority of his employees, all surrounding none other than Sarpanch, who was speaking in a booming voice:

'You people speak of quitting the company and taking back the papers you signed upon employment, and forget to remember the positions we were in two years ago! Think of the situations we were in! We did not have proper shelter, proper clothes, a sufficient bank balance, any water, any crops—and, in spite of all our issues, that kid made the decision to cultivate the crops in a better way than had ever been before and to come to our rescue, like a god! What are we to him? We're merely outsiders to him. And yet he still he treated us like a family and shouldered the burden of our bad days.

'On those dark days, we were in trouble, and now, he is in trouble—so we should repay the favour and join our hands with him! We would be going against God to leave him alone today. We were like babies—unable to fend for ourselves—, and he helped us to walk along with our grief. He never left any of us behind. Please, let us shows our humanity; let us join hands and show Swaraj how he allowed us to run, and get him back on his feet!'

Swaraj could have collapsed from shock: this was Sarpanch, Swaraj's first obstacle in creating his company, who had stood against and ridiculed him from the onset of his business ventures.

The crowd, completely unaware that the object of their discussion was right there, linked hands and began singing the national anthem in unison. *This*, Swaraj thought, tears trickling down his face, *is why I wanted to help the people.*

He waited until the end of the anthem before he started clapping, and, after turning around and noticing Swaraj, Sarpanch sheepishly approached him.

'Your business is wonderful,' Sarpanch conceded, 'and you now won't need to worry about your workers deserting you: our rain god will be with us soon. Your workers love and respect you, and will follow you no matter what.'

Swaraj, still tearing up and filled with newfound hope, thanked Sarpanch profusely, feeling as though his mind had been cleared of any previous fog or demotivation.

To top this off, Swaraj received a message from one of the clients he tagged in his social media post regarding the company's state, and a meeting through video call was arranged between the two. Word spread amongst Swaraj's workers of such a development, and it was as a result of this that Chandru messaged Swaraj to give him the heads-up: *They're all waiting for your words, Swaraj. I have also been contacted by the famous actor Mr. Yashas, and he has offered to share his knowledge for developing the lake. I've also been contacted by someone with a PHD, who educates students on social welfare; however, he had more of an interest in agricultural studies specifically. We'll be seeing both soon.*

Over the next few days, such meetings were attended to with these figures; and, as if by magic, the more the matter got discussed, the more the clouds seemed to darken with the promise of rain. The aforementioned actor indeed possessed a variety of thoughts concerning the development of lakes in and around the village, and he detailed a plan in the form of a blueprint to solve the issue. In return, he asked the people of the town to join hands and work together to ensure the project's completion.

As the days passed, a cool breeze surrounded the village; and, on one blessed morning, a drop of rain fell in the hands of Swaraj—then another, then another, until finally the rain came down like a thick curtain.

Everyone in the street started to dance for joy, some of them opening their mouths and turning up their faces to get a taste of the glorious water. Swaraj joined them, and in that moment, he was sure he'd never felt such joy in his life: everything was now falling into place. Everyone was caught in the ecstasy of their rain dance.

After everybody had calmed down a little and Swaraj was going to head home, the actor pulled him to the side and asked if they could meet in Swaraj's office. Once they had arrived there, the actor immediately began speaking.

'You are a very big financial consultant in this area,' he began, 'and have a lot of potential, and yet here you are working, as a common man, leaving both your parents and Avani.'

Swaraj felt his own eyebrows shoot up. He could only assume Chandru had told the actor about his state of affairs in his personal life. Meanwhile, little to swaraj's knowledge, Chandru was actually outside the office door and, having heard Avani's name, suddenly pulled back the hand that was about to open the door, instead choosing to listen outside for a moment. However, the door was opened anyway as the actor had gone to leave, and both Swaraj and the actor smiled as they saw Chandru's reddening cheeks as realisation dawned that he was eavesdropping. The actor thanked Swaraj for his time and promptly left, Chandru saying nothing and quickly walking away in embarrassment.

The next day, Project Lake was commenced, everyone harbouring high expectations for such a plan. Further, as word spread even more about the project, additional nearby villagers came to Swaraj and offered their aid in the project, which Swaraj agreed to readily. Furthermore, to kickstart the project, Mr. Vihaan (the PHD-holder and lecturer) dedicated a one-hour session to educating the villagers on the procedure and the ways in which they were to implement the latest technology.

Armed with both hope and newfound knowledge, the villagers got to work, and, after just fifteen days, everything on the blueprint had been completed. There was only one requirement left: rain. Indeed, it had rained for the entirety of that first day, and yet it was now ten days until the rain season was over and there hadn't been a drop more.

It was decided that, the following day, all the villagers would go to the temple to offer their prayers to the god Indra Deva. The entire village agreed, knowing full well that if no rain fell by the end of the season, they may very well be doomed for the next eight months.

Somewhat inappropriately, Swaraj silently started to laugh as the villagers began talking about this. Chandru turned to him, frowning and asking him what he found so funny.

Swaraj shrugged. 'I just know Lord Indira Deva will end up coming on the last day of raining season.'

Chandru shook his head. 'What on earth has brought you to that conclusion?'

Swaraj smiled knowingly. 'Because every time there's some sort of life-changing situation in my life, it changes on the sixtieth day—and that correlates with raining season's end.'

Chandru wasn't convinced, and still felt very anxious about the situation. Swaraj, on the other hand, was confident in his prediction, and was still smiling as he walked away, calling, 'Time will tell!' over his shoulder.

Chandru stood for a moment, counting the days in his head: indeed, on the fifty-ninth day of the drought, the sun had shone down on the village with no sign of rain; and, surely enough, the following day had been when the village had been blessed with those sheets of rain. *Even still,* Chandru thought, *it's too flimsy a theory to rely on.*

CHAPTER ELEVEN

Swaraj had travelled to his parents' house and, after having a bath and eating his breakfast, Swaraj sat with his parents, expecting the topic of Avani to arise; however, his mother never uttered a word about the matter, likely rightly assuming that it was a sensitive subject.

After he had eaten, Swaraj got ready and biked to Avani's branch, finding that the bank was filled with customers upon his arrival. The noise from the counters clanged in his ears, and he pushed his way through the throng of the crowd in search of Avani—almost an impossible task as each cash counter was surrounded by people.

Suddenly, a lady came up behind Swaraj: 'May I help you?'

Swaraj nodded. 'Yes, I'm looking for Avani? She works here.'

The lady smiled sadly. 'I'm sorry, sir, but she left this job a while ago.' Swaraj frowned. *Surely not?* '...but if you have any service queries, I can help you.'

Swaraj was dumbfounded, his mind having gone blank. Quickly excusing himself, he pushed his way back through the crowd and stood outside the door, wracked with confusion. Hoping for some clarification and a clue as to Avani's whereabouts, Swaraj messaged Satish: *Avani has left her job at the bank. Do you know where she is?*

A minute later, a message pinged back: *No, I had no idea she'd even left.* Swaraj's heart sank. Slightly panicked, Swaraj entered the bank for a second time, grabbing the lady's attention who he had just spoken to. 'Excuse me!' he called, and she turned around, plastering a smile on her face upon seeing Swaraj. 'Sorry to bother you again, but by any chance did you receive any kind of indication from Avani as to where she'd transferred to?'

'I'm afraid I don't remember, sir,' the lady responded apologetically. 'I joined here on the last day of her notice period.'

Thanking her hastily, Swaraj swung back out the doors and sped to Avani's house. His heart in his throat, he rang the doorbell and waited ten seconds, thirty, one minute, two minutes... nobody came to open the door. He rung it again, and again, and again, to no avail: he heard none of the usual voices echoing from inside.

Feeling at a loss, he was about to leave when he saw a neighbour emerge from her own house. She seemed rather harsh-looking and moody, and yet Swaraj didn't care: he needed to know where Avani was.

Somewhat rudely, Swaraj called, 'Excuse me, but do you know where Avani is?' He indicated to the door. 'She used to live here. We're colleagues—well, we were. Same bank, but a different branch.'

The woman shrugged non-committedly. 'They left here a while ago.' She eyed Swaraj apprehensively. 'Said they were moving near to the industrial area.'

The industrial area was huge. He'd never find her there.

'Do you have their address?' Swaraj asked, unable to keep the desperation from his voice.

'No.'

Swaraj felt like a shell of a man. His eyes filled with tears, and he felt torn between heartbreak and anger: she *had* left and said *nothing*.

Gruffly thanking the woman under his breath, he got back on his bike and went back home. For the rest of the day, he ate nothing, his mind racing with thoughts of Avani—thoughts that continued in his dreams when he finally managed to fall asleep that night.

Despite his night of broken sleep, he got up early the following morning, immediately trying to call Avani's mobile only to find his number had been blocked. Desperation and anger coiling in his stomach, he then called Satish, explaining the situation to him before breaking down again.

'Try not to worry yourself, Swaraj,' Satish soothed. 'I'm sure she's fine, and that she tried to contact you. It'll all have just been a big misunderstanding.'

Swaraj heard his friend's words but didn't believe them for a second: Avani simply didn't care for Swaraj as much as he did her. Swaraj had never felt so betrayed.

'Listen,' Satish said, cutting into Swaraj's thoughts, 'I'll call you in half an hour or so; I need to go and look into some things.'

Swaraj thanked him and hung up the phone, and began staring at the wall opposite him, his mind running circles. Perhaps Avani *had* wanted to contact him.

Perhaps her phone had broken, or her new husband didn't want her contacting him.

Before long, thirty minutes had elapsed, and Swaraj's phone rang: Satish.

'Swaraj, I think I've done it: I've found Avani's address.'

Swaraj almost dropped the phone. Before he could say anything, Satish continued, 'I'll message it through to you now so you can go see her.'

He hung up the phone. The call had lasted all but forty seconds, and yet Swaraj's mood had altered completely in just that time: he'd be able to see her.

Swaraj hadn't even showered, but he didn't care: he sped out the house and biked to the placed Satish had messaged to him.

Within a few minutes, out of breath and suddenly exhausted, he paused by the side of the road for a second, and all he could do was listen to his own heartbeat and breaths. It was as he stood there gathering his own thoughts that Avani emerged from a nearby building, like a goddess he had summoned. For a moment, they just stared at each other. There she was, before him, as though she'd never even left.

Unsure what to do, he smiled. She smiled back. It felt like they were meeting for the first time again: so much had changed for both of them. They both began to walk towards each other and, when she was right in front of him, Swaraj said, 'Hey.'

Avani's eyes seemed to dance. 'Hey.'

There was a lump in Swaraj's throat he had to swallow. He motioned to the back of his bike. 'Want me to drop you at your place?' He paused. 'Like the old times?'

The smile disappearing from her face, Avani shook her head. Swaraj's heart sank: things between them felt so different.

'Come on,' he insisted. 'You can't walk all that way.'

Avani looked at him for a moment, Swaraj unable to read her expression, the emotion in her eyes. Finally, she exhaled. 'Okay.'

A few minutes later, her arms were wrapped around Swaraj's waist as they sped through the busy streets. For a few minutes, they had sat in complete silence. Finally, Swaraj spoke.

'So, what's the big story behind you resigning from work?'

Swaraj couldn't see Avani's face, yet he noted the wobble of emotion in her voice. 'I was forced to leave.' Swaraj heard her swallow. 'The bank needed to focus more on cross-selling than bank operation, so there kind of wasn't a place for me there anymore.' She took a breath. 'Have you taken leave from work to come here today?'

'No,' he responded simply. 'I left my job and came here to resume my study.' He shrugged. 'I was also in a pretty low place when you rejected my proposal, so I didn't know what to do except to leave my job and come back here.'

There were a few moments of silence, and Swaraj wished desperately he could see her face. After some time, Avani sighed and said, 'Stop the bike; I'll go by bus.'

Swaraj's heart sank: had he stepped out of line by mentioning the proposal? As per her wishes, he pulled to the side of the road and made the bike skid to a halt. Without a word, she dismounted the bike and stalked away. Swaraj, filled with panic yet again, locked the bike hurriedly and ran after her, he pulled her back by her hand.

'May I know why you don't want to speak with me anymore?'

To Swaraj's surprise, Avani's face was contorted with anger, her voice shaking with pure rage. 'Have you gone *mad*?' She snatched her hand out of his grasp. 'I *never* expected this from you.'

'Avani, please, what have I done?' Swaraj asked, his voice breaking. To his horror, all of Avani's anger suddenly seemed to dissipate, instead taking the form of tears: she crumbled to the ground and began to sob. Swaraj crouched behind her and folded her in his arms. 'What's going on, Avani?' he murmured into her hair. 'You can talk to me.'

'The day you left my house,' she began, 'the groom's family and the bride came to see me. The parents liked me a lot, and so took my details to show to their astrologer so they could match me with their son, Kundali—who is significantly older than me.'

With these words, the puzzle pieces began to slot together in Swaraj's mind: Avani hadn't been the one getting married that day.

Avani continued. 'They fixed the date for the potential wedding, and, after they left, my parents asked my opinion on this. I rejected the idea completely: the age difference was too big. Everybody started to scold me, with the exception of my brother, who stood up for me and stated that he agreed with me.' Her breath was shaking. 'Everybody fell into silence, and my brother then told my father he should at least take some time to let me get me head around such things.' She then looked up at Swaraj, her eyes so sad yet so beautiful. 'I couldn't tell them actual reason for my rejecting him: the sadness in your eyes when you saw me that day—not because you loved me, but because you cared for me.' She sighed. 'I don't believe in love-based marriages—they only ever result in divorce—, and yet somewhere in my gut, I began to realise I had started to like you.' She blushed slightly at these words. 'But, alas, my parents would never approve of our union now, as you now have no job and have resumed study.' She shook her head. 'My parents aren't getting any younger, so they won't wait for you. They want to be relieved from their duties as soon as possible.'

Swaraj was speechless: suddenly, he had everything he'd prayed for—Avani's heart—, and yet this now seemed to mean nothing. He would never get Avani's parents' approval. It was then that his conversation with Chandru from that morning popped into his head.

'Can you give me sixty days, Avani?' She frowned in confusion. 'Sixty days, and I promise I'll be in front of you with a job offer. Another thirty after that my parents will be in your house, discussing our wedding with your parents.'

Avani shook your head. 'I swear you really have gone insane.' She sighed. 'But if you're saying you can sort your affairs in that timescale, then I'm willing to take a chance. But if you fail to do so, the choice will be out of my hands: I'll be forced marry somebody else.'

The thought sickened Swaraj, but he agreed nonetheless, confident in the fact that he'd have a job by then. They then headed back to Swaraj's bike and resumed their journey and, when they were a few blocks away, Avani asked him to stop, took out her phone, and unblocked his number in front of him. She then got off the bike.

'I'll get the bus from here,' she said. 'It's only a few minutes' journey, and I don't want anyone seeing you.'

As she began to walk away, Swaraj called, 'I love you, Avani.'

She looked over her shoulder, smiled, and continued to walk. Swaraj felt on Cloud Nine.

He wasted no time in fulfilling his promise: the following morning, he set off to his uncle's residence in Bendalpura to search for a job. Bendalpura was a very wealthy, well-turned-out area, and the majority of companies had their regional offices and headquarters there.

He had already phoned his uncle regarding any local job opportunities already, who had referred some consultants to him, providing him with a list of job openings. He contacted each and every company for a job, the majority of them offering him a job but for far too low a wage. His weekdays were spent like this, searching for a suitable job high and low, only stopping during the weekends, when he would go back home and spend time with his family.

CHAPTER TWELVE

It had been forty-five days since Swaraj's conversation with Avani, and there was still no sign of a job. Every day that passed, he'd tick a day off his calendar, his anxiety creeping higher and higher.

On the morning of the forty-fifth day, he came back from yet another unsuccessful. To his surprise, his cousin opened the door to his uncle's house before he could do so himself, and immediately asked, 'If you end up getting a job, will you be moving elsewhere?'

Swaraj was confused and slightly uneasy. Unsure how to respond, he laughed and said jokingly, 'I'll move if you can find me a job!'

His cousin didn't smile, instead thinking in silence. Swaraj excused himself and shouldered his way into the house, as his phone had just started ringing: Avani. She had begun calling on a daily basis for updates on his job hunt, also taking the opportunity to remind him of the amount of time he had left—the number creeping lower and lower.

Another ten days passed, and Swaraj received a message from the Pvt Sector Bank: he needed to attend an interview. Thus, he began to freshen up, all the while silently praying to God that this would be the one, the one that would prove successful, the one that would get him out of this rut and allow him to have Avani for his own.

He arrived at the interview on-time and, before going in, promised to himself he would give this one everything he had. Thus, that's what he did, and at the end he was informed that he would receive an update within the next few days. Thanking them and keeping his prayers in his thoughts, Swaraj left. This was potentially his last shot before time was up.

Finally, the sixtieth morning commenced, Swaraj having left his uncle's and returned to Ramagiri a few days before. He had heard nothing from his latest job interview.

Meanwhile, the entirety of the village seemed to be holding its breath in anticipation for rain—Chandru even more so, as Swaraj's confident words concerning the rain falling on this day echoed back to him.

Ignoring the aching in his heart, Swaraj came to the office, quickly sighting Chandru and calling him into his office. Chandru, though confused, obliged, trailing Swaraj as he entered the office and closing the door.

Once in the office, Swaraj turned to Chandru. 'You seem to be more tense than usual today, Chandru,' he commented.

'Yes,' Chandru responded simply. His tone was rather accusatory. 'You haven't been properly responding to any of my questions; I feel like I've become an outsider to you.' He sighed sadly. 'It's because of this that I wish to quit this job and leave this place. Clearly I'm not a friend to you anymore.'

Swaraj shook his head, offering him a seat and a drink of water, which he accepted gratefully. 'Why are you so upset with me? You're my friend; you've remained by my side throughout the many stages of this company.' He took a breath. 'I promise I'll open up more at some point, but that'll come with time.'

This seemed to trigger something in Chandru, for he then arose, muttering something under his breath about not having more time to waste. He headed to the door, and Swaraj, realising there was nothing he could do to talk his friend around, shrugged.

'There are some places in the village where rainwater is accumulating, so get the village ready today—and kindly inform the team members that I need their work completed the by 6pm today.' He examined his nails. 'We'll resume work as usual tomorrow.'

Chandru paused and eyed Swaraj with contempt. Swaraj, however, seemed like he couldn't care less. 'Just till 6pm,' he shrugged, 'and you will to come to know of my past.' He then shouldered past Chandru and left the room.

Chandru, despite his irritation and frustration at his friend's treatment, did as he was told, informing all the employees that they should come to the lake at 18:00. He felt Swaraj was being overconfident—cocky, even—, and so he relayed Swaraj's message with sarcasm, explaining that rain was expected today and so that the lakes would be filled.

The news spread like wildfire, and, before long, every villager was talking about Swaraj. As the day wore on, scepticism rose: there was no sign of any clouds emerging anytime soon. As a matter of fact, the air was thick with heat, and every farmer quickly agreed that if rain didn't come today, they would revoke their agreement with him.

This news reached Swaraj as the clock hit 17:30, and, one-by-one, the villagers began to surround the lake, waiting for the promised rainfall.

The sun started to set, everybody anxiously checking their watches, the time, the clouds. Before long, it was almost 18:00, and Chandru approached Swaraj, smiling smugly. Swaraj took out the file containing the land papers signed all those years ago.

The minutes elapsed, and there was still no sign of rain. At 17:59, a cool breeze started, piercing the warmth, and the crowd started to chatter: dark, angry clouds began rolling over the horizon until the sky looked like a thick blanket of darkness. It was at 18:00 exactly that the first icy cold rain droplet shivered from the sky, followed by another, then another, until the blissful water was coming down in sheets.

Feeling as though he could cry with happiness and relief, Swaraj received a call from one of the Pvt Sector banks: he had been selected for the company, and he was to collect his offer letter the next day.

Meanwhile, the eyes of the villagers, mirroring the sky above, filled with tears of joy, all one-by-one bowing their heads and kneeling down in gratitude. One of the villagers, who had retracted his land loan the day before, hurriedly went to Swaraj and gave the file back, going to touch Swaraj's feet in thanks before Swaraj stopped him, instead enveloping him in a warm, loving hug.

Similar events unfurled with Chandru, for he came to touch Swaraj's feet but was quickly absorbed into a hug instead, both men crying with joy. As the men embraced, Swaraj closed his eyes and imagined what his future would entail now, and, after unwrapping himself from Chandru's arms, he broke free from the crowd and called Avani.

'Hello?' came her voice. It was low, devoid of hope: she clearly was not expecting any good news.

Swaraj could barely speak, he was smiling so widely. 'Mrs Swaraj, prepare the food, for your fiancé Mr Swaraj has got a job with a decent salary. He will be posting in Bendalpura.'

Swaraj immediately had to yank the phone away from his ear as Avani was screaming with joy. He then disconnected the call and, as the rain continued to fall, he then called his cousin and told her to pack his bag, for he would be moving to PG from next week. She immediately began to cry, apologising profusely for her previous mistake before both began to dance for joy in the rain.

Chandru quickly joined in, as did, slowly but surely, the rest of the village.

The rain persisted heavily for the entirety of the night, almost all the lakes' water levels being raised to the max and, as planned, the water was quickly stored, the village priest, along with Sarpanch, quickly draining the lake water the following morning for future use.

All the village's inhabitants quickly followed the same procedure, each of the houses quickly being renovated as big tanks were installed for rain water storage—some for drinking, some for practical use.

Big sumps were installed to store the rainwater, pipes then being attached to direct the flow. The installed sumps had a capacity for 200 litres of water storage.

Swaraj swiftly made it a compulsory mandate for all the villagers to have such a system installed in time for rainwater harvesting: all rainwater would be directed to the sumps, the motor being fixed so as to move the water from sump to tank. The tank water would then be used for bathing and for washing utensils. All the costs for such a system were to be covered, with the exception of any minor repair works.

The villagers were now in a position to redeem some portion of their savings via their mutual funds; even the stock market on that particular year provided better returns for their investments. Swaraj also continued to offer employment to the citizens of the village—an element of Swaraj's character that made him into an idol in the eyes of the villagers, his water purifier strategy giving him more of an identity in the village than ever before.

CHAPTER THIRTEEN

After the summer, the rainy season started, and this year they had sufficient water for storing and cultivating. The lakes were filled to the brim, and, as time pushed on, Swaraj decided to plant a tree in front of all the village houses, and began planting a tree each time one was cut down. Swaraj had established such authority in the village at this point that all the villagers didn't even think to say no to him. He had become a family member to them.

Five years passed, and the company had reaped huge amounts of profit. Every year, Swaraj introduced one top-up facility for his employees, all of which being paid generously. News started to spread amongst the nearby villages—news that eventually reached the CM. Swaraj's agreement with the CM had been for a five-year period, and so the time for renewal was imminent. Swaraj swiftly informed all his employees of this, and arranged for a meeting with them all regarding the agreement.

All the villagers assembled at the meeting place, Swaraj logging into the meeting via video chat. Every person in the hall quickly stood, and Swaraj, blushing slightly, told them to sit back down, that he was just one of them. Not wanting to disappoint him, the villagers quickly obliged, and, after a few moments of silence, Swaraj began. He commenced by first stating the word of agreement, then explaining that, in three days, the agreement was due to come to an end.

'Thus,' he finished, 'you will all need to give back the amount you initially provided, and can revoke the land papers.'

Everybody eyed one another, tension filling the room. Finally, Sarpanch stood.

'I'll not give you the amount back,' he declared. 'Instead, I will give my personal money, and continue as an MD for this company. I do not want this company to shut down, for it has done too much good. We do not want the land: we need a guide, a well-wisher, like you.'

The crowd had elapsed into silence, as had Swaraj: he was speechless. Slowly, chatter started rising from the crowd, murmurs of agreement sweeping across the hall.

The decision of the villagers quickly came to light: Swaraj was to continue as an MD for the company. The villagers were not willing to take back their land—and, to prove this, one of the villagers stood and began speaking.

'Before Swaraj came, I was living in a dark room. Even when sun rays fell on my path, it was as though I had been blinded: left to navigate the world as half a soul. But after your arrival, you have cured my vision, and shown me a path of light.' The man's eyes filled with emotion. 'I was having to take loans I knew I wouldn't be able to pay back from the bank. Even subsidy was unhelpful to me. However, all of this changed when you gave me five lakh rupees, took over my land, and gave me a job. Today, the value of five lakhs has inflated to that of ten, and my family is secured for health benefits, my son and my daughter are studying in a city school, and I am now receiving a consistent salary every month.' The man smiled widely. 'All my family are healthy and secure, something hugely important for me and my wellbeing. You have saved over two hundred families similar to yours, and, if emergency ever strikes, I know my bank balance is able to take care of us.

'Earlier, we had to go to the bank for everything; now, those from private banks are asking us for *our* services. Even our leaders failed us in times of desperation, and yet you have done it.' He was properly crying now, making Swaraj also cry. Chandru, who had stood beside him during the meeting, rubbed Swaraj's shoulders soothingly, and, after having a quick drink of water, Swaraj addressed the crowd.

'My intention has been to maintain transparency in all my policies,' he stated. 'Some may be willing to take back their land, and others may not—hence, why I called for this meeting. If you are all happy with the work I have done here, we will work together for a few more years.'

Everybody jumped for joy and shook hands with one another, and, long after he had logged out of the conference, tears still continued to roll down his face. It was then that Chandru sighed and turned to him.

'I am sorry for losing faith in you, Swaraj.' He sighed. 'I will not ask you any more questions about your family, and, when the time comes, I hope you will share any experiences you have with me. I have pestered you for your thoughts confidence, and have taken on the chin the lesson you have taught me.' He then hugged Swaraj tightly, adding more emotion to the day.

The following morning, Chandru arrived at Swaraj's house, only to find he was not available. *Perhaps he has gone to the factory,* he reasoned. With this in mind, Chandru wandered to the factory, only to find Swaraj was not there, either.

Chandru suddenly felt himself tense, and, somewhat frenziedly, began to search everywhere for his friend, to no avail. Chandru quickly informed one of the villagers of their leader's absence and, word spreading, the whole day was spent searching for Swaraj, from dawn till dusk. There was no sign of him anywhere.

The next morning, Swaraj went back to his house to find that there were two hundred families waiting to see him. Dumbfounded, Swaraj pushed through the crowd till he found Chandru,

'What on earth is everyone doing here?' he demanded.

Chandru flushed. 'Everyone thought you had gone missing, so everyone decided to camp in front of the house and wait for you.'

Swaraj sighed, directed an apology at the crowd for not informing them of his whereabouts, and headed back inside, asking Chandru to come with him: they needed to talk.

Chandru, feeling very important as he trailed Swaraj and the rest of the crowd dispersed, entered the house. After being offered a drink and a seat, Swaraj began speaking.

'The other day, before the rain started to fall, you questioned me on my background,' he began, taking a sip of water. 'And I think it's time I told you.'

And, from here, Swaraj filled Chandru in on all his recent personal events: how Avani had accepted his proposal and started making daily phone calls again; how Avani's father had received a call from his cousin regarding the marriage proposal, and how he had told him that Swaraj was abroad and well-settled, and that Avani now only felt able to accept half-heartedly; how Swaraj had called his dad and directly told about Avani and the life he had planned for them both after their marriage; his father agreeing to the union but telling him not to worry about it until his brother's marriage had been done.

'It was this weekend that I spoke to Avani's parents about the wedding, and it was after this that Avani turned cold, claiming she'd be degraded in the family for our marriage, for I had gone into real depth over my feelings for Avani. I responded that it felt as though she was using love as a marker of status in society, after which I hung up.'

Swaraj then explained that he had been in a dilemma, unsure who to approach for help. He had then called Avani's mother directly. Her tone had been warm and polite upon answering, and, encouraged, Swaraj had begun speaking: 'I love your daughter and wish to marry her, but I have not yet asked her, despite us being good friends. I have informed my parents of my wishes, who have consented to the union. It would be greatly

97

appreciated if all of you could decide your own thoughts on such a prospect and let me know; I'll come and speak to you this weekend.'

Avani's mother had then simply told Swaraj to come this weekend so they could all speak. Swaraj had felt as though a physical weight had been lifted from his shoulders.

Sunday had arrived quickly, Swaraj arriving at Avani's house, as invited. Her parents has quickly taken him under their wing and treated him with respect, quickly offering him a refreshment and a seat. Upon sitting, Swaraj had said, 'I know for any parents this is a very difficult situation, and yet you have still given me the chance to express my feelings—something I'm eternally grateful for.'

He had then gone on to explain how he had loved Avani since their first meeting, and that he had been praying ever since then that she would be his.

'I would care for her deeply,' Swaraj had continued, 'and it would become my primary goal in life to fulfil her views, her wishes, and her dreams.'

Both parents had listened to Swaraj's words delicately, and it was decided that the couple would decide between themselves for the next couple of days, and would call Swaraj when they had reached a decision.

Three days had passed, and, as promised, Swaraj received a call from Avani's father, who greeted him as his son-in-law. They had decided they approved of the marriage.

'I had never felt happiness like it,' Swaraj said now, face glowing in remembrance.

Swaraj had then gone on to discuss the matter with his father, who was disappointed over the matter being discussed again: he had made it clear he didn't want it brought up until Vaibhav's wedding was done with. However, Swaraj had pressed on with the topic in his excitement, and, apprehensively, agreed to meet with Avani's parents the following weekend to discuss the wedding.

During this visit, Swaraj's father politely but firmly explained Vaibhav's imminent marriage, and that he would prefer for Swaraj to properly restart his career and get settled before discussing the prospect of marriage.

'Vaibhav's marriage is next year,' he had explained, 'so we can do Swaraj's then, too.'

The details of this meeting had been relayed onto Swaraj by his father after the event, and, shortly after, Avani's mother had called Swaraj.

'Your father has informed us he wants you to "settle in" into your new residence and job, and as much as we'd love to be able to say otherwise, we are currently not in a position to wait for such a timescale.' Swaraj's heart had sunk as he digested the words. 'She is already approaching the age of marriage, and we wish to be relieved of our parental duties sooner rather than later.' we also have to complete our duties when we are fit and fine, better you settle in life and then think of marriage, but sincere request is to do not commit any hazard, we always will be with you.'

This concluded Swaraj's narrative, this conversation having occurred the night before. His heart still felt heavy, and he couldn't help feeling some resentment towards his father: if he hadn't said anything, Avani would still be his.

Now the conversation from the night before was fresh in his mind, Swaraj, after Chandru had departed, decided to call his father. He relayed the previous night's conversation before saying, his voice threaded with disappointment, 'They're now probably going to look for some other man for the marriage. You *knew* they would.' His voice broke as tears rose to his eyes. 'Thank you for that, Dad.'

Before his father could say anything, he ended the call and spent the rest of the day with a heavy heart, Avani's face being all he could see. The thought of her marrying somebody else was soul-destroying, and yet he couldn't see a way out of the situation: the circumstances were exactly as Avani had predicted all those months ago.

One sleepless night later, Swaraj got up and was getting ready for work when, at 11:00, he received a call from Avani's mother. Pressing the receiver to his ear, her mother began speaking quicker than he could say hello.

'We will wait for your brother's marriage,' she said simply. 'However, if your parents do not approach us about the matter at that time, we will marry Avani to somebody else.'

The call disconnected, and Swaraj's eyes glistened with newfound hope: perhaps all would work out after all?

With that, Swaraj and Avani continued with their daily calls, and Swaraj's business continued to thrive. Before long, he received an invitation for Vaibhav's wedding, and, of course, he booked the day off work immediately so he could go.

When there were just a few days left till the wedding, Swaraj was on the phone to his parents, discussing the wedding and the guests that would be coming.

'I suppose it'll be a little strange to see Avani's parents again,' Swaraj said. 'It's been almost a year.'

Swaraj's father was silent for a moment and, when his voice came through the receiver again, it was laced with discomfort. 'We actually didn't invite them. I didn't think it necessary.'

Swaraj frowned, already feeling highly embarrassed: what kind of impression would it give to Avani's parents if his own family didn't invite them to his brother's wedding?

'We'll invite them now,' his father said quickly, likely spotting his error in judgement. 'Although if you want us to because you still plan on marrying Avani, I don't think that would be for the best. Marrying for love never ends well.'

Swaraj felt betrayed. His father pressed on. 'Swaraj, you're not even capable of paying one month of your rent. How can you expect to lead a healthy *marriage*? You and your wife would both end up being our burden.'

Unable to control his temper, Swaraj raised his voice. 'Do *not* compare this to other love marriages,' he snapped. 'I'll have you know we've planned our future very well, and won't be needing your assistance. We will be in Bendalpura and will manage our daily expenses independently; we won't ask you for a single rupee.' His voice shook with pure rage: they would *not* take this away from him. 'If you are not willing to consent to my marrying Avani, this will be the last day you get to call me your son.' Tears sprung to his eyes. 'If you need me, you can call me and I will come home, but it will be with Avani, my wife.'

With that, he disconnected the call and packed his bags for Bendalpura. Wasn't every parent supposed to support their children? Why was it Vaibhav received all the support in the world, and yet when it came to his happiness, he had to beg and plead?

For the entirety of his journey to Bendalpura, anger still bubbled in his chest to the point where his whole body tensed and, after some time, his head began to ache.

It was a couple of days after this phone call—two days of trying to forget his father's words—that Swaraj received a call from no other than his father.

As Swaraj pressed the phone to his ear, he opened his mouth to tell his father he didn't want to speak to him—but his father began talking quicker than he could speak.

'Your mother and I have talked,' he said, 'and, considering Avani's parents have accepted your wishes of marriage, we don't feel in a position to stop you. If you come over this week, we can meet her officially in her house—as we've arranged with her father... your future father-in-law.'

Swaraj's heart, which had felt leaden and heavy for some time now, suddenly lightened. He thanked his father profusely, promising him he wouldn't regret his decision, before hanging up the phone—only to find he had a missed call from Mrs Sita Lyer, Avani's mother. Swiftly calling her back, she immediately began speaking.

'Do you think your parents have agreed to the marriage for your sake, or because they genuinely think it's a good idea?'

'They genuinely support it, I think,' he responded honestly. 'Have you been informed of our planned visit this weekend?'

'Yes. I look forward to discussing the marriage further.'

The arranged date arrived quickly, Swaraj having arrived at his parents' the day before. Avani was thrilled to bits upon their arrival, overcome with joy that the journey to their marriage had officially begun. Now they had both families on-board, they were officially engaged, and, over the course of the visit, it was decided the wedding would occur in six months' time.

The happy couple, after this meeting and Swaraj had to return to work, continued with their daily calls, all the while counting down the days till their marriage.

CHAPTER FOURTEEN

Before long, the blessed day was upon them. The day passed blissfully, the ceremony being a small, modest one with both sides of the family and some friends present. This was everything Swaraj had wanted since he had first laid his eyes upon Avani, and yet he still found himself blinking back tears after the ceremony: they still were not living together, and Swaraj still had his work to attend to. They would be just as separated as before.

Chandru tried his best to console Swaraj, despite his confusion: this was the one thing he thought was guaranteed to make his friend happy, and yet here he was, borderline hysterical still.

Chandru was still trying to calm Swaraj down when, to the men's surprise, Mr Yashas—the actor who had provided aid to Swaraj's company when it was in danger of shutdown—entered.

'Congratulations on your marriage,' he said uncertainly, sitting beside Swaraj and patting him on the back warmly. 'I have brought with me a gift—one which will hopefully be of good use to you for a long time.'

Swaraj surveyed Mr Yashas, unsure: the man didn't have anything in his hands. Mr Yashas then leaned forward and closed Swaraj's eyes for him, and, suddenly, the weight on Swaraj's chest lifted, a cool breeze seeming to stroke Swaraj's cheek and a white, comforting light filling his mind. It was after a few moments of this that

Swaraj felt a new presence beside him, and, without opening his eyes, he could feel it was Avani. He addressed his wife.

'Avani, I can't leave here without you,' he conceded, his voice breaking. 'I really love you, very deeply.'

He got down on one knew and opened his eyes. Silent tears were trickling down Avani's face, tears of happiness. Wordlessly, she slipped her engagement ring from her finger and placed it into Swaraj's palm. 'I wear this so I feel like you're with me. Now, I won't need such a reminder, because you'll actually be here.'

With that, she knelt beside Swaraj on the ground and embraced him, Chandru and Mr Yashas grinning with happiness: this was the lady behind all of Swaraj's success. Once the couple stood back up again, they found Mr Yashas now had a young girl in his arms.

'I gift you your daughter, Ayushi,' he said, placing the girl in Swaraj's arms. 'It is now your role to take care of her: she has missed you very much.'

Swaraj embraced his daughter and kissed her on the cheeks, new tears—tears of fatherly love—now springing to his eyes.

'Thank you, so much,' he said to Mr Yashas, who smiled warmly in return. 'I now have all the family I need. Please take care.' Handing his daughter to Avani, who buried her nose in her daughter's hair, Swaraj turned and embraced Mr Yashas, who squeezed him back before waving farewell.

For the rest of that beautiful day, Avani was introduced properly to all Swaraj's family and friends,

Ayushi, upon seeing Chandru, taking his hands and murmuring, 'Thank you very much, Uncle; you have cared for my father.'

Chandru, speechless and deeply touched, simply stroked her cheek and said, tears in his eyes, 'Only the most wonderful of personalities possess this kind of quality. You are just like your parents.' Swaraj and Avani gazed proudly upon their daughter. 'And if in the future you ever need it, I will take care of you as well.' He delicately kissed her forehead.

It was at this time that Swaraj's phone chimed with a text message from Mr Yashas: all were invited to his place for dinner. All agreed, and, after the food—the wonderful, delicious food—was served, Mr Yashas asked Swaraj about his project and how it was coming along, to which Swaraj responded with pride.

'All is going amazingly. We still need to make some additional improvements—we're planning for a digital solution. I need a techie.'

Mr Yashas nodded. 'I'll call Aryavardhan once I'm back and will update you. He'll be what you need.'

'Thank you, my friend.' He shook his head. 'You've been an incredible help for my business and family.'

The following morning, Swaraj awoke with the dawn, Avani and Ayushi—his new, beautiful family—rising shortly after him. After everybody had freshened up, Swaraj provided both his girls with a tour around the village, their new home. The happy threesome went to the lake—built by Mr Yashas—, both adults playfully splashing their daughter as she squealed with delight. The hours passed in a blur, and it was only as the sun began to sink behind the horizon and the air had a biting chill that they wandered back home. It was whilst on their way that they came across Chandru, who greeted them warmly.

'How do you find the village, Avani?' he enquired, turning to Swaraj's wife.

'It's perfect,' she responded. 'It's full of greenery, and I saw lots of families here. They all seem so happy.'

The only issue with the village was that, even though it was financially independent due to Swaraj's farming business, its citizens still relied on the outer cities for education—meaning all its young citizens had to make a long commute daily for school. This was something Avani explained as an element of concern for her—especially as the prospect of Ayushi growing older dawned.

'This is a large reason why we've requested for Arya—Aryavardhan—to come. I have some plans regarding this.'

Right on cue, Swaraj's phone started to ring: Arya. Avani and Chandru couldn't hear the conversation from Arya's end, and Swaraj remained silent, intently listening, until the end: 'Thank you, Arya. Let's do this.'

He hung up the phone and Chandru turned to his friend. 'Shall I arrange for a video chat?'

Swaraj smiled. 'Yes please, my friend.'

Aryavardhan arrived bright and early the next day, who was greeted warmly by Swaraj and his family. Avani quickly fetched him a glass of water upon his arrival and Ayushi unashamedly threw herself onto him for a hug, asking if he'd brought any chocolate.

'A little fairy told me there was a young lady here who liked chocolate,' Arya said to Ayushi, taking a slab from his pocket. 'That's why I bought your favourite!'

The little girl took the chocolate, delighted, and kissed him on his cheeks in thanks before running off and showing her mummy.

Before long, there was another knock at the door: Chandru. Swaraj introduced him to Arya and the men shook hands jovially. Once everyone had their refreshments and were settled, Arya addressed Swaraj.

'So, my friend,' Arya begun, taking a swig of water, 'Mr Yashas told about your project. I think it sounds wonderful, and I hope there is more success and abundance waiting for you in the years to come. So, what is your next move?'

'All in good time, my friend,' Swaraj smiled, snuggling down into his seat. 'For now, let us enjoy one another's company, and we will talk business tomorrow. I'm sure you would like a rest after your journey.'

And, indeed, he did: the man fell into a deep slumber soon after his arrival, and it wasn't until the following morning that their business resumed with a knock on Swaraj and Avani's bedroom door.

Swaraj got out of bed, wrapping a dressing gown around himself and opening the door to find Arya stood before him, in his workout clothes.

'Fancy joining me for a morning jog, my friend?' he enquired, pointing out the window, where the sun was rising. 'It's a beautiful day for it.'

Swaraj agreed that it was, and, before long, the men were jogging around the perimeter of the village, Swaraj showing him all his favourite spots, as he had done with Ayushi and Avani a couple of days before.

During breakfast an hour or so later—once the men had both showered and slipped into their day wear—, Swaraj asked Arya what he thought of the village.

'It's a very nice village,' he responded. 'Thanks to your business, it's nice and green—although there are some smaller regions that still need help.'

'I have a plan for that, too,' Swaraj said, taking a bite of toast. 'As much as the company is doing well, I'm planning to start the school with advanced technology.'

Arya frowned in apprehension. 'How are you going to go about starting that...?'

Swaraj shrugged. 'Well, I'm going to need to meet the CM and discuss it with him. I've already booked an appointment to see him in an hour or so, if you'd like to come.'

Arya agreed enthusiastically, curious to see how Swaraj would introduce such a proposal. The men finished their meal, Swaraj kissed his wife and daughter goodbye, and they both headed off to meet with the CM.

Within minutes of them arriving, the CM opened the office door from which they had just arrived, saw them waiting, and invited them into his space, offering them both a chair.

'Now, what brings you here today?' the CM asked, folding his hands in front of him and waiting expectantly.

Swaraj took a deep breath and, with the support of Arya, detailed everything in his plan, from his overarching vision to the intricate details. The CM kept a neutral expression throughout Swaraj's talk, and yet he was inwardly impressed, and, as soon as Swaraj had finished, he fished the relevant paperwork from his desk and pushed it to Swaraj with a pen to sign.

'It sounds like you have given this a lot of thought,' the CM observed, leaning back in his chair. 'Your plans are promising, and I've seen what you have already done for this village. You have my complete support in such a venture.'

Swaraj shook hands with the CM gratefully and thanked him for his faith and his time, and, upon quitting the building, Arya offered his congratulations, admitting that it really did seem like a good, solid plan. Swaraj then quickly messaged Chandru and asked him to arrange for a video chat as soon as possible. Three minutes later, a message pinged back: *Done. I have also told the villagers of an imminent meeting.*

Swaraj suddenly felt a wave of appreciation for his friend, who seemed to now have implicit trust in his friend's plans whenever they occurred.

The two men then headed back to Swaraj's house. Swaraj quickly greeted his wife and daughter before heading to his office and logging onto the video chat—to find that all the villagers were already there, all waiting curiously for their emergent leader's words. Swaraj, overcome with feelings of support and gratitude from the villagers, began to speak.

'Thank you all for coming on such short notice—although hopefully this announcement will be worth your while!' He smiled at all the people. 'I will be soon working with the government to reopen a public school in the area, after some technological advancements have been made. Each and every child of this village will be invited to join the school so they won't have to make the lengthy and expensive trip to the city.' There was an excited chatter in the hall.

One of the villagers raised their hand. 'Will I be able to pay the fees for grandchildren, too?'

Swaraj shook his head. 'There won't be any fees: it's a government school.'

'Yes, I know,' the villager responded, 'but you will be investing in a digital platform, and I think all us villagers would want to repay you by contributing to that in any way we can.'

There were murmurs of agreement in the room, and Swaraj was rendered speechless: he hadn't expected a penny from anyone, and yet here they were, wanting to repay him off their own backs.

Swaraj finally spoke. 'If you really want to pay the fees, we have a trust fund, which you can donate into if you please. However, please know there's no pressure from me or anyone else to do so.'

The villagers all instantly took turns putting themselves forward for the trust fund, and it was whilst they were sorting this amongst themselves that Swaraj thanked them all for the last time and logged out of the call.

Swaraj emerged from his room and relayed the meeting onto Arya and Avani, who were just as awestruck as Swaraj had been. One thing was clear: the villagers were completely committed to Swaraj and his ideas.

'Who will be the teachers in this new school, though?' Arya asked. 'We'd have no staff for such a venture; we'd need to spend some time just advertising for trained professors.'

Swaraj simply smiled and responded, 'Do you remember when we were young, when we were going to school on the morning of an exam, I was crying for fear of failure, before a lady—a transgender lady who I recognised for being the talk of the city since her transition—came and comforted me? She gave me confidence right before I was due to sit the test. She told us her name before she left: Kanchana.'

Upon hearing the name, Arya's eyes sparked in recognition. 'Yes, I remember.'

Swaraj was almost jumping with excitement, and Arya and Avani exchanged a surprised glance at one another. 'I wasn't there, so I don't know,' the latter shrugged.

Arya ignored Avani and said to Swaraj, 'But where on earth could we find her?'

Swaraj shrugged. 'I have no idea, but we have to find a way as soon as possible.' He then remembered a similar event that had occurred years later, this time right before a Mathematics exam when Swaraj had been fifteen. A lot had rested on the results of that exam: if he were to fail it, his parents would likely scold him and view him as a public disgrace.

Right in the nick of time, Kanchana had come to Swaraj to comfort him, like an angel, or a goddess: she had dried his tears with her delicate hands, and now, Swaraj murmured the word she had said to him: *We should not be afraid of the people around us; the only person we can trust and let go to is the man inside you— your own self-confidence. If you are confident, you can achieve anything. Be bold, answer those questions, have faith in yourself.* She had then walked away, smiling encouragingly over her shoulder.

Now, Arya and Swaraj looked at each other helplessly, racking their brains for ways they could find her. Arya was clueless, but it wasn't long before a memory sparked in Swaraj: nobody else had known, but Swaraj had actually invited Kanchana to his wedding weeks ago: it felt like the least he could do after all her help. However, he had received a response shortly after: *I am grateful for and touched by your invitation, but we are disconnected from such traditions: my family members would not approve. However, you are very good to me, and I do not wish to cause your family discomfort. You know what the public thinks of people like me.* And, true to her word, she had not attended the ceremony.

Swaraj had done so via letter: during one of their pre-exam meetings, Kanchana had provided him with her address in case he needed any extra mindset help before a test. He still had her address stashed somewhere in his office.

Some hours later, after Arya had departed and both his wife and daughter were in bed, Swaraj penned a quick letter to Kanchana, simply asking if they could meet up. Not wanting to waste any time, he slipped out the house and delivered the letter right to her house.

It was early the following morning that Swaraj saw his glimmer of hope from his living room window, wandering through the streets—likely searching for Swaraj, as he had not put a return address on the letter.

Reasoning that his wife would likely remain in bed for a while, Swaraj shrugged on a coat and ran right after her just as she was turning a corner and about to disappear from sight. Breathless and tired by the time he'd caught up. Going to speak before quickly realising he was too out of breath to, she turned, smiled at him, and said, 'You're the first person who has tried to meet with me again.'

Catching his breath, Swaraj answered, 'I just wanted to come and thank you: I scored higher in those tests you came to me before than I ever have in any other subject. I surpassed everybody's expectations—mine included.'

Kanchana was touched by Swaraj's gratitude, and was about to respond when her gaze settled on something over Swaraj's shoulder. Swaraj, suddenly chilled to the bone, knew without even looking who it would be.

Avani stood behind them, rage rolling off her in waves.

'You want someone like *that* to be a teacher?' she spat. She strode toward her husband, her eyes filling with tears, and, as Swaraj began to attempt to console her, she snatched his hand away from her and slapped him across the cheek, hard.

Swaraj stared at his wife in shock, clasping a hand to where he had been struck. It was then that Swarna, a friend of Kanchana's Swaraj had met once before, emerged: Kanchana hadn't come alone, probably due to her anticipating such a situation unfurling.

Kanchana said nothing, simply observing the scene with sad eyes. It was Swarna who intervened: she stood between Swaraj and Avani, addressing Swaraj calmly.

'You have a very good wife, Swaraj,' she said delicately before turning to Avani, 'but please don't raise your hand to him again: speak with mouth rather with hand, and we can express our feelings productively.' She smiled warmly, and Avani's cheeks burned with sudden shame.

'You're welcome to come to our house and we can treat your face,' Kanchana suggested, turning to address Avani. 'You're welcome as our daughter-in-law, too.'

Sheepishly agreeing, Avani quickly fetched a sleepy Ayushi before the fivesome made the short walk to Swarna and Kanchana's home. Avani remained quiet and, whilst Swaraj complimented them both on their house, Avani looked around in silent admiration, as did Ayushi.

'I have taken up private teaching to some of the community members,' Kanchana said. 'Most of them requested ICT lessons, after which some of them went abroad to continue their studies.'

Avani raised her eyebrows in surprise and, admittedly, admiration. 'How is it you were able to do all these things?' she asked suddenly.

'The same reason anyone can,' Kanchana shrugged. 'I have a PhD. Although you wouldn't know it, with how I am regarded by society. It doesn't bother me anymore, though.' She smiled warmly, as though showing she forgave Avani without explicitly saying so. Avani blushed again. 'I used to feel down about it, but not anymore: one must adjust to such situations. After all, everybody is born with something or other that they feel insecure about, but that's often where I come in: along with academics, I try to teach young people how we can maximise our potential and explore the world by believing in ourselves. It's only from that point that we can healthily compete with other people.' She thought for a moment. 'I'm actually doing a lesson in Vidyapur Forest a little later. You're welcome to join.'

The rest of the room—even Ayushi, who, abandoning all tiredness, had been running around the house in excitement a few moments before—went silent as Kanchana spoke, and it was from this moment that, despite Avani's initial uncertainty, Swaraj knew he had made the right decision.

'Kanchana,' Swaraj said in a low voice, 'someday soon, I'm going to come to you and ask for a favour—one that you would enjoy. Can you promise me that when the time comes, you won't say no?'

'Of course, Swaraj,' she said without a moment's hesitation.

Later on that day, Swaraj called Arya and told him to meet him at his house. He obliged without asking why, assuming it was something to do with the teaching position, and simply followed Swaraj when he led him to Vidyapur Forest.

Upon arrival, Swaraj explained, 'Kanchana is here, teaching to the forest people.'

Indeed, as though they had summoned her, they emerged from a thick of trees to find Kanchana seated on the ground. She was around sixty-five years old, and yet she still had the essence and energy of someone forty years younger. The two men watched for a while as she coached the people surrounding her for half an hour or so before they all departed, Kanchana then turning around and spotting Swaraj. She expressed her happiness at his coming, and her and Arya exchanged a warm embrace; she had remembered him from his younger years perfectly.

It was from that point that Swaraj explained his plan to Kanchana, as well as his wish for her to be one of the teachers. She listened intently and her eyes glimmered with anticipation by the end of his explanation.

'I'll try my plan here first and, if it's successful, there's no reason why not we couldn't go global,' Swaraj concluded, Arya nodding rigorously beside him. 'I need more people on-board first, though—hence our asking you. This will hopefully lend the way to more job opportunities for the people. Places like Bendalpura are in high demand for education and work, and, if I can start building such government schools across the nation, nobody will have to leave their hometowns for work and education.'

Kanchana shook her head in awe and pride. 'This is what will allow the people to obtain true independence.' Her eyes glistened. 'You have become the people's freedom fighter.'

It was after this discussion that the trio wandered back to the village so that Swaraj could show Kanchana the government school he hoped to reopen, which was currently undergoing renovation. Indeed, the building was, for now, rather derelict: there were rooms without roofs and doors, and some without walls. It was here that Swaraj turned to Kanchana.

'How would you feel about being this school's principal?'

Kanchana embraced Swaraj, jumping for joy and, of course, agreeing to his idea: it was the kind of thing she'd always dreamed of.

CHAPTER FIFTEEN

The renovation took surprisingly little time, and was eventually built to be a modest yet facilitating size: twenty rooms with good-quality benches, computers, and all the suitable equipment. Upon its completion, Swaraj wrote a vacancy post in both the local paper and on social media, on which he already had quite a large, esteemed presence due to his community work.

Surprisingly, applicants for the post did not stream in as quickly as Swaraj might have hoped, although not all hope was lost: the students were ready and eager.

In order to give the school somewhat of a social standing, Arya created a website for the school, allowing for online applications, payments, and details of the facilities offered. To top this off, he additionally created an app for mobiles linked with a range of E-Marketing companies for promotion purposes. Finally, the school's address was made available, residents in the school's catchment area being targeted particularly for promotions so as to ensure of their awareness of the school's opening.

Eventually, Swaraj extended his advertising ventures to people outside his village and to Garudadri, one of the neighbouring villages. He additionally commenced the interviewing process of some of those who had applied to be teachers, and yet emerged from each one with no luck: all of them were motivated purely by the money, and not by the prospect of teaching and inspiring masses of young people in the same was Kanchana was. Swaraj additionally wanted his teachers to be aware of and proficient in the marketing arena, but this was absent also.

After posting a new school recruitment advertisement on social media, he received some applications for the position a few days later. Interviews were arranged, during which his main objectives for the school (i.e., to provide knowledge applicable to anywhere; to teach the students in an innovative way; and to be viewed as a real competitor by other schools) were run through. Is it happened, it was these interviewees that possessed the qualities Swaraj had wished for in his employees, and they were promptly given the requested role. Salaries were fixed, and directions were given to the school.

Shortly after this, Swaraj, Avani, Arya, and Sarpanch arranged a meeting, in which Swaraj explained the school's current situation, as well as its mission and objectives; he also stated his idea of allowing for the illiterate and innumerate women in the village to join the school along with the younger students, which the other three agreed to and was advertised for swiftly.

Having heard of Swaraj's new scheme, the young people from Garudadri who had gone abroad for studies returned to the village, all of which Swaraj took under his wing.

As a result of all of the above, the building was quickly renovated and ready, the students were available and eager to begin, and the teachers were all employed and well-trained—and yet Swaraj hadn't yet chosen a date for the school's first day. Because of this, Arya and Swaraj took it upon themselves to book a meeting with the CM to kickstart the inauguration of the school.

Leaning back lazily in his chair, the CM shrugged, 'Maybe, but only if I can share some of the company's profit.'

Swaraj, initially thinking he'd heard wrong, felt a wave of rage crash over him: all of this work and he had done nothing, and he was expecting to receive a chunk of the profit? Angry yet unable to see any other way out, Swaraj reluctantly agreed. Now that he thought about it, the CM rarely spoke to him over any matters besides those to do with money.

At that moment, the CM's personal assistant arrived, apologising hurriedly for the interruption before murmuring something to the CM about the election campaign. It was then that Swaraj had an idea.

'Mr CM,' he said quickly, jumping to his feet. 'If you allow for the inauguration of the school, I will campaign for your election: I will tell my villagers to vote for you as CM for the next tenure. I'll even tell them you were behind the school project.'

The CM was taken aback and eyed his PA apprehensively, unsure how to respond.

Leaning down to whisper in the CM's ears, Swaraj heard the PA murmur, 'Please accept, Mr Shakuni: he has a very good social standing in the village. There'd be no need to campaign for elections.'

The CM, his mind made up, happily agreed. Swaraj could have punched the air. Upon exiting the meeting, himself and Arya discussed its contents incredulously, surprised at how self-centred one man could be. At least one good thing had come from it: the school would now be able to start. Swaraj quickly messaged Mr Yashas, filling him in on the state of affairs and inviting him to the school's opening.

The day of new beginnings arrived rapidly, all the people of the village gathering around the school in a gaggle of anticipation. The education minister and Mr Shakuni, the CM, also came to witness the institute's opening. Mr Yashas arrived to the group shortly after, eyes glimmering with excitement, and, as per the agreement, Mr Shakuni was the one to cut the tape, light the lamp, and say a speech.

'Considering I have been the backbone of all these developments within this village for some time now,' Mr Shakuni was saying, smirking slightly, 'I ask all of you to vote for me in this upcoming election. Thank you.'

The villagers remained silent upon the speech's completion, some of which turning to Swaraj, confused, who stood next to Mr Shakuni. Noting the crowd's adverse reaction, Mr Shakuni blushed slightly and walked from where he had been stood on the stage, this embarrassment only heightening when Swaraj was the only one clapping. Mr Yashas could hardly contain his laughter, and Mr Shakuni, face now a deep red, trailed away sheepishly. The villagers had, of course, all known who was really behind all the recent progressions, and yet they all slowly began to clap out of politeness, following Swaraj's lead—as always. Some shouted out that they'd vote for him still, somewhat alleviating Mr Shakuni's mortification.

However, the crowd wasn't completely in good humour: Mr Shakuni had still been the one to cut the tape and light the lamp, not Swaraj. Thus, due to the restless of the people, a new strip of tape was hung and a new lamp brought out, and Swaraj did the honours, to the delight of the people. The crowd all began to join hands and jump for joy, and Swaraj felt highly emotional and deeply touched: this was what this had all been for.

Before long, Arya had managed to make the school website and app available internationally, on which all services and classes were advertised for—including the classes for the women of the village and the newly proposed evening classes for the farmers interested in studying. Within lessons, Swaraj also ensured the villagers were educated in regards to money management, Arya also proposing and taking up politics classes. Mr Yashas joined the trust as a Director, Swaraj became the Treasurer, and Arya and Avani became Trustees.

Furthermore, Arya and his team created unique ID numbers for each of the students, and Swaraj created bank accounts for the students and the farmers—the latter so they could transfer whatever amount they were able to to the school trust fund. For excluding Fees for the school were collected on a person-by-person basis depending on their yearly income, as follows:

- Income from 1 to 5 lakh P/A = 0.5% P/A

- Income from 5 to 10 lakh P/A = 0.75% P/A
- Income from 10 lakh and above = 1% P/A.

Meanwhile, donations were collected as follows:

- Income from 1 to 5 lakh P/A   = 1% P/A
- Income from 5 to 10 lakh P/A = 1.75% P/A
- Income from 10 lakh and above = 3% P/A.

The aforementioned fee and donation rates were also applicable to the Garudadri villagers, who had also agreed to pay the relevant fees for their children. Furthermore, students were admitted not on the basis of grades, but on the basis of their interests and their motivations. Thus, any student could join: any race, any gender, any background. The school was the most inclusive and well-run for miles around.

Security cameras were shortly installed in the school to ensure students' safety, which would be constantly active during school hours and able to identify the specific ID numbers within the school through GPRS tracking. Furthermore, all accounting/monetary matters were governed by Avani and Swaraj.

Arya created the workflow as student will be joined, they will get their UID number, bank account will be opened for student, fees will be paid by student through their account, GPRS and CC camera will be live, and accessibility will be shared only to the respective parents. Parents will install the app or they can create the User ID in the website, once logged in student GPRS will be active, location will be shared, later they need to select the camera, and their son or daughter will be visible, even parents can also log into the classroom to check the quality of education. Mobiles for the students will not be allowed inside the premises of the school building; mobile identification device will be activated.

All exam papers and other necessary materials were made available on the school's website and app, login details being distributed to all students. Further, any needed basic stationery was additionally readily available within classrooms, and the school office was always contactable via any means—whether that be video chat, phone call, or text message.

Swaraj named the school The School of India.

CHAPTER SIXTEEN

Shortly after the inauguration of the school, Swaraj received a call from an unknown number. He accepted it and pressed the phone to his ear. 'Hello?'

The voice that came made him almost collapse in shock: it was the Prime Minister.

'I just wanted to say congratulations for all the splendid community work you've been doing in your area,' he said warmly. Swaraj's hands were shaking. 'I don't suppose you could come to my office in Delhi soon, could you? I would like to discuss some matters with you.'

Of course Swaraj agreed and thanked him profusely for his time before calling Avani and Arya and excitedly relaying what had just happened. He invited them both to come with him to meet the PM, and both agreed instantly.

As always seemed to be the case as of late, the day Swaraj both couldn't wait for and dreaded had arrived. He couldn't wrap his head around being given such an opportunity, and he was terrified of making a bad impression or saying something out of turn. However, Avani and Arya were massively supportive both in the build-up and when they were on their way, wholly focusing on calming his nerves before arriving.

It was whilst they were anxiously waiting for the PM outside his office that security strutted over, bringing none other with them than the PM himself. He smiled at

Swaraj, introduced himself warmly, and offered him a gentle handshake, then inviting the him into his office: the other two were kindly requested to stay outside.

'Is there any way they can come too, sir?' Swaraj asked politely. 'They've been just as involved in the process as I have.'

The PM, surveying Swaraj with a glimmer of admiration, agreed, and, as the foursome entered and got settled, Swaraj quickly formally introduced himself and said, 'Please bear with me during this meeting; I'm rather nervous.'

The PM just laughed jovially and told him not to worry. He then quickly sobered and began to talk seriously.

'So, Swaraj. My biggest congratulations for your recent ventures: I hear you have been extremely successful during your agriculture and school projects respectively.' The PM leaned forward and held Swaraj's hands in his, smiling warmly.

'And to you, sir,' Swaraj said. 'Your terrorist attack prevention missions have been a great source of relief to countless people.'

The PM simply smiled and offered them all coffee for all of them, who all accepted the refreshments gratefully before the PM continued.

'Swaraj, the work you have taken upon yourself to do is highly admirable, and as much as I know you have earned the peoples' respect and that they will continue to support you indefinitely, I wish for more support for you.'

Swaraj said nothing, instead continuing to listen intently. His heart was pounding and his hands were clammy.

'Swaraj, I would like you to join my party and help me in my mission of aiding the nation. I admire your agriculture project highly, and would like to implement it all over the country.'

Swaraj was utterly dumbfounded and immediately turned to Avani and Arya in shock; however, neither of them looked even remotely surprised. *They expected this. They knew the potential of my work.*

They smiled warmly at Swaraj, Avani offering a thumbs-up in approval, and, tears in eyes, Swaraj accepted the PM's offer. And just like that, Swaraj was the CEO and Innovative Director of Farma India Pvt Ltd, approved by the PM to be implemented in each and every part of the country as soon as possible. Upon his own request, the PM also paid a visit to the village so he could properly observe the workings Swaraj had established— and it was during this visit that the PM became even more passionate about altering the current school and agriculture situation within the country, renaming Swaraj's school 'Swadesh Public School' upon leaving. The citizens were all massively inspired, and the whole ordeal felt like a massive victory for the village.

Suddenly, everything from the past few years came flooding back to Swaraj: his meeting Avani for the first time; his initial proposal of his business idea and how he was ridiculed; his grandmother's death; the business's booming success; his winning of Avani's heart; his and

Avani's wedding; Ayushi's glorious entrance into their lives; and, now, his opening of a school and working alongside the Prime Minister. It was what dreams were made of.

It was whilst Swaraj was reflecting in such a way that a memory came back to him he didn't know he had: a memory from just after Avani had given birth, the moment that had subconsciously kickstarted his establishment of the school. It was in the hospital ward, a small girl, aged around six, emerging from one of the rooms, tears streaming down her pale face. She had run straight for Swaraj, shouting, 'Daddy!' in a tormented voice. Quickly after, a woman had emerged, chasing after who Swaraj presumed to be her daughter, crying in a similar fashion and quickly lifting her daughter, burying her face in her hair.

'I need *Father!*' the girl had screamed, shivering uncontrollably. 'He promised me I'd join a good school, and now he's sleeping.'

Swaraj had felt numb as he watched the scene before him, his mind blank. It was then that a nurse had followed the twosome, to which the mother rushed over to quickly. Swaraj had only just been able to hear the nurse's words: 'The amount of poison he took was too much. I am afraid he is no more.'

The woman had absolutely crumbled, and Swaraj, stumped for what to do, had offered the young girl a piece of chocolate, his newborn daughter in his mind, giving her a quick hug. Her mother had smiled weakly at Swaraj and thanked him.

He later found out from the talk of the village that the farmer and his family had been from Ramagiri, and that the man had drunk the poison as a result of two years of crops not yielding enough sufficient returns, ultimately leading to him being unable to clear any of his loans. The young girl's words had echoed back to him in the following days—*He promised me I'd join a good school*—that ultimately inspired him to set everything into motion. Swaraj had treasured Ayushi even more than he knew possible after this event, Avani feeling the same after he had relayed the story onto her, too.

After he had told Avani what had happened, he had said: 'If tomorrow were to be my last day of existence, I would be filled with regret, for I feel I haven't achieved anything of true value. I want Ayushi to be proud of her dad.'

And so, he had taken up the Swadesh Project— something he had proposed to his wife before saying, 'I need your support: I want every child and parent to be and to feel secure.'

And the rest had been history: Swaraj hadn't so much as looked back once since, until now.

It was directly after Avani and Swaraj had such a discussion filled with reflection that Swaraj's phone began to ring: it was the Prime Minister.

The ensuing conversation was over within a matter of minutes, after which he turned to his wife. 'The PM is coming over tomorrow,' he said, shaking his head in disbelief: how had this become his life? 'He wants to discuss something with me, it seems; he told me not to tell anybody.'

Avani frowned. 'There must be something unexpected going on,' she responded. Swaraj, meanwhile, was already messaging Mr Yashas, simply asking him to come over the following morning urgently. He responded almost instantly in the affirmative.

CHAPTER SEVENTEEN

Swaraj had been plagued with insomnia for the entirety of the night, his mind running in circles: why had the PM been so urgent about meeting him so last-minute? And why so much secrecy? The questions were endless, and, the following morning, Swaraj was borderline delirious with exhaustion: he hadn't had even a minute of rest. He felt wholly unprepared for such a meeting.

Shortly after Swaraj had given up on sleep and got himself ready for the day, Mr Yashas rapped at the door, his face the picture of concern.

'Is everything okay?' he asked immediately.

Before Swaraj could respond, a familiar figure came racing towards him from the distance, their expression one of utter bewilderment: Sarpanch.

'Swaraj!' he was shouting, almost tripping over his own feet. 'Swaraj, there's a *helicopter* about to land!'

Despite his own anxiety, Swaraj managed to keep his voice calm. 'Relax, Sarpanch,' he soothed. 'All is well: I'm expecting a visitor shortly.'

Avani emerged from the house with Ayushi bundled in her arms, summoned by the commotion. It took one glance between the couple for Avani to understand what was happening, and she smiled encouragingly at her husband.

Avani, Swaraj, Ayushi, Mr Yashas, and Sarpanch all left in the direction of the sound—which, sure enough, eventually led them to a helicopter that had just landed and, naturally, a colossal crowd of villagers. The crowd was charged with curiosity and shock, the same questions being flung around repeatedly: Who on earth could this be? What is happening? Should we run? Despite their awareness of the PM's involvement in the village's schemes, none of them expected him to be the person to step out—and, when he eventually did, the crowd elapsed into shocked silence.

Hurriedly shouldering his way through the crowd, Swaraj quickly made his way to the helicopter and promptly shook hands with the PM, welcoming him warmly. The villagers were simply stunned, their mouths gaping open like fish. Unknown to Swaraj, the news of a mystery arrival had spread to a neighbouring village, and, slowly but surely, the residents from there began to stream in, too.

Thankfully, the Prime Minister had brought his security guards, who surrounded both the PM and Swaraj and ensured their safety as the crowd grew more and more hectic and packed. Chandru, Arya, Mr Yashas, Avani, and Ayushi quickly managing to break free from the clump of people, Swaraj quickly informing the PM that they would need protecting, too, which the security guards quickly did upon the PM's instruction.

Upon arriving at Swaraj's house, the security guards and Swaraj's friends were all asked to remain outside whilst the men had their discussion. It was only Swaraj's family—Avani and Ayushi—that were permitted to come inside, but only on the strict condition that they remained in a different room. Swaraj's anxiety suddenly climbed to an all-time high with these words: this was clearly serious business.

After refreshments were provided and both men were settled down, the PM immediately cut to the chase, opening the conversation by taking a pen drive from his pocket—a pen drive, Swaraj recalled, that Swaraj had given to him during their last meeting. It comprised all the unethical activity Swaraj had uncovered: notably, the records of illegal money that had been brought into the economy by the CM.

'Myself and my team have investigated the contents of this pen drive thoroughly,' the Prime Minister said gravely, not breaking eye contact with Swaraj. He then motioned to the TV in front of them. 'Would you mind putting on the news channel?'

Swaraj quickly obliged, and was shocked to see that the CM's house was headline news: IT officials were raiding it—along with those of his employees—and terminating their leases on their properties. To Swaraj's surprise, the PM shook beside him in silent laughter.

'Again, I offer my congratulations, Swaraj,' he said, his eyes twinkling. 'You have done our people a great service for bringing this to the limelight.'

Swaraj was unable to respond: he thought he had gone into shock.

'After the opposing party inevitable forces the current CM to resign from his role, I want you to take over his position, because I want you to be leading from the front. Any decisions I make will go through you first, and you will be one of the chief decision-makers within society.' He took a sip of water, likely to allow this to sink in. 'You haven't been afraid to break the rules in the name of doing right and helping the people, and I need hands like yours in every state so that we can change the opinions toward the discriminated within our nation.'

Swaraj could feel his eyes growing wider and wider the more the PM spoke. 'I'm planning on making some very big changes within our system in the next few years,' he pressed on. 'And with your help, we can achieve such needed changes. I need you, and so do the people.'

Swaraj was completely lost for words: he didn't know what to think.

It was then that the door to the room they were in swung open and Ayushi threw herself in like a mini hurricane, wrapping her arms around her father's neck, squealing with excitement. She had clearly been listening at the door, and yet the Prime Minister didn't seem to mind this: in fact, he was laughing in delight at the little girl, his eyes filled with affection. Ayushi then released her vice-like grip from her father and bounded over to the PM, taking his hands in hers and thanking him. Then, with surprising maturity and sincerity, she began to speak.

'My mummy used to tell me one story about my father whenever we had dinner or lunch: she would say he was a person who likes to accept new challenges, especially those helping those nearest and dearest to him.' To Swaraj's surprise, the PM's eyes began to glisten with tears. 'He was always away when I was younger doing work, and my friends at school used to rag me around, badmouthing my father and telling me he didn't care about me. But then he proved he could do the impossible, and so I would tell them all with pride that he was my father, and there was nobody like him.'

Tears sliding down the PM's cheeks, he smiled warmly at the little girl, squeezed her hand, and kissed her gently on the forehead. Swaraj was, yet again, rendered speechless: he'd had no idea his little girl held him in such high regard.

It was then that Swaraj felt another presence behind him and, upon turning around, there was Avani, her eyes similarly filled with pure emotion. Ayushi then ran into her arms, after which Avani wordlessly wandered to her husband's side and lay a hand on his shoulder encouragingly.

It was then that Swaraj finally mustered the words to speak. 'Sir, I accept your words with more happiness than I have ever known, and I am so extremely grateful to you for believing in my work.' The PM smiled. 'However, I still have some things I would like to discuss with you, if such a plan were to be carried out.'

And with that, the discussion was carried out, Swaraj's daughter and wife lovingly by his side. After around half an hour, the conversation was closed, and the family emerged to the swarms of people along with the PM.

'Thank you all for waiting so patiently,' the PM said, a hush falling over the crowd.

The PM then began to walk, the crowd parting for him, the security that had been stationed outside, as well as Swaraj and his family, following. The crowd respectfully dispersed, each person heading back to their respective homes. The PM then took out his phone and called no other than the CM, politely asking him to arrange for a meeting and an important announcement.

'Please ensure the stage is set and ready within an hour. I'll be roaming the village in the meantime.'

Whilst this was done, Swaraj and his family—as well as some unexpected news reporters—showed the PM around Swaraj's factory, proudly showing him the intricately designed machines and tools created for improvising the crops. He then took him to Swadesh Public School, where he congratulated Swaraj yet again on his achievement whilst still providing constructive criticism. As he had done with the factory, Swaraj talked him through his vision and the inner workings of the school, also showing him the Swadesh app Arya had so diligently worked on. The men also talked through Swaraj's planned updates and future objectives before wandering to the fields and going through the technology used on them to boost the agriculture.

Soon enough, the hour was up, and the PM had been notified of the stage being set and all being ready to go. Before the foursome could set off, one of the media people who had been trailing the group asked, 'Mr Prime Minister, what do you have to say about the IT raids across the state?'

The PM simply smiled and said, 'These are just workplace dramas.'

The cameraman laughed. 'Sir, what is your next move?'

The PM shrugged. 'If my party came into rule, the news wouldn't be filled with things like this; it would be filled with news of development, of facts and figures.' He sighed. 'When it comes to the next election, we will not campaign aggressively: instead, we'll just be showing to the people what we prioritise and let them decide for themselves whether that's what they want.' He then smiled, an almost mischievous spark glinting in his eye. 'And the person who I hope the people will be voting for is Swaraj here, who has done endless good for his community.'

As soon as these words were uttered, there came a clapping sound: the words the PM spoke were being broadcasted live across the nation, and the villagers in their houses had begun clapping. This sound only grew louder as the group approached the stage that had been set up for the PM's meeting, and, upon entering, the crowd were surely enough all on their phones watching the news. The clapping had reached a deafening roar when the PM shouted for them to stop, to no avail. Noticing the PM's struggle, Swaraj simply waved his hand to the audience and the crowd immediately elapsed into silence. The PM glanced at Swaraj in surprise, and it was in that moment he knew he'd made the right decision.

The PM stepped to the stage and began. 'I'm sure I don't need to introduce you to the wonderful man who stands beside me. It is with his aid that I plan to make this village into even more of a development project than he already has.'

From there, he explained his new financial plan.

'In forty-five days, I will be banning the old notes of the Rs500 and Rs1000 denomination across the nation: you have been given this time period so you can exchange all your notes through the bank. Don't worry, the banks have been informed of this in advance, and they are prepared for large-scale note exchange demand across the nation. This is all with the aim of demonetising black money. New notes will be made available to all banks from tomorrow morning. Any monetary injustice ends here.'

EPILOGUE

The CM watched the news report unfurl with burning cheeks, and, within minutes, there were people stood outside his home, shouting for him to resign.

He hadn't ever seen this coming; he thought everything had been kept under wraps. He didn't know whether to be relieved or enraged.

The CM quickly grew bitter as his reputation spiralled and he became unable to control his resentment: everywhere he went, he was tormented for his lies, his selfishness, his lack of leadership. Before long, he came across as unhinged and explosive in the media.

When he awoke one morning a few weeks later to the usual abuse and taunting, he knew he would not be able to handle the pressure for much longer. He booked the first ticket to Rajyabhavan to hand in his letter of resignation.

It was a new era: an era of utterly transparent, selfless, innovative leadership. An era of prosperity. An era of all start-ups.

ACKNOWLEDGEMENTS

In memory of my grandparents, the late Mr Raghavendra Char and M/s Sharada Bai, and with blessings for my grandparents Mr Nagarajachar and M/s Rathna Bai.

There are two most beautiful people in this world: my father Mr Sujanendra and my mother Suvarna. I do not have the words to express my feelings to describe their love towards me.

I also thank my birth place, Mysore, for giving me culture and the opportunity to live a wonderful life. I am very happy to thank and send my best wishes to my brother Mr Vibhudendra and my sister-in-law M/s Pooja, and Anish.

There are not the words to thank the most iconic person, advisor and companion: my wife M/s Archana, who has stood next to me throughout my difficulties and encouraged me to start a new career as a novel writer. Not forgetting my father-in-law Mr Ramesh and my mother-in-law M/s Girijamba, who have encouraged me to stand as a fighter during my difficult days. They are also in my heart as my parents. I thank Yashas, my cousin, who ignited the spark in me to enter into this world of writing.

I also convey my thanks and wishes to my aunt M/s Dr Deepika Pandurangi, Mcom and Phd, who helped during the first stage of my editing phase. She is an author of the famous book "Adarsha Sthree Rathnagalu", written in Kannada. She is a motivational speaker and has taken up a new venture as "Kannada Dimdima", which is a workshop to motivate and give guidance to all people, including students, with regards our culture and values in Kannada literature.

Not to forget the most important person in my life, M/s Hayley Paige, the Head Publishing Consultant and creator of Notebook Group, and author of both fiction and non-fiction, including her upcoming non-fiction "Entrepreneur Book Success". Thank you for assisting me in editing, publishing and marketing my novel, "Swadesh: The Age of Startups". I also extend my thanks to the entire team at Notebook Publishing, i.e. all of those involved in sales, editing, marketing and publishing.

I thank all of those who have come into my life from my bottom of my heart. I have taken much knowledge and many experiences in my life and penned these into a story. Thank you to all.

TO BE CONTINUED...